SPIRITUAL WORLD WAR

By - EMMANUEL N TSHUMA

Pharos Books

©Publishers

Publisher: Pharos Books (P) Ltd.
Plot No.-55, Main Mother Dairy Road
Pandav Nagar, East Delhi-110092
Phone: 011-40395855, +14049995474
WhatsApp: +91 8368220032
E-mail: sales@pharosbooks.in
Website: www.pharosbooks.in
Edition: 2021
Printed By: Sushma Book Binding House, Okhla
Industrial Area, Phase II, New Delhi-110020

Spiritual World War
By- Emmanuel N Tshuma

Contents

Acknowledgements

I would like to thank my family and relatives for their support in helping me writing this book. I thank The United Pentecostal Church for grooming me ever since I was a kid as well as for teaching me the word of God since Sunday school until I was an adult. I was able to use those teachings in my life to continue living for The Lord.

I would like to extend my gratitude to The Global Vision Ministerial College and Clergy Council which also taught more on The Word of God eventually helping me in getting my diploma in Biblical Theology.

Last but not least. I would like to thank my Christian friends for their continuous support as well as my workmates in the military.

Dedication

I would like to dedicate this book to 4 categories of people.

- Everyone who is a Christian or who wants to be a Christian
- Every religious person
- All religious leaders
- All people working in the military

Preface

'Spiritual World War' is a Christian book written by Emmanuel N Tshuma. It gives a clear picture on what is actually happening in the spiritual world, there is a war that is taking place. It is very unfortunate because we live in a physical world and we are unable to see these things happening but if you are spiritually alert you begin to realise that there is a battle between good and evil. This takes us back to the creation story. God created the Heaven and the earth. After creation, we saw the fallen angel, 'Lucifer' who is called 'the devil' or 'Satan' confronting Eve into eating the forbidden fruit.

After eating the forbidden fruit, Eve gave the fruit to Adam who ate as well. That is the first case in which we see the relationship between God and man distracted. This means there is a problem and we as human beings have to find a way to live right without being tempted by the enemy. The fallen angel was cast out of Heaven into the earth with his angels and they have since claimed to dominate the world. They are everywhere in the world doing their best to blind the eyes of man so that they do not know that there is an everlasting God who promises eternal life when we follow Him. This means we are in a spiritual world war that happened in the past and will still happen in the future until judgement day comes whereby God will be putting an end to this war. One of the important aspects that we must look at is that the opposition team is already defeated and it is clear that during judgement day, they are going to be cast out into the lake of fire. Their motive is to take as many people as they can before that day comes.

It actually means that we should be careful with this world war, people who are weak are going to be easily convicted by the enemy, he is real and is living in the spiritual world, we cannot see him but we can see the weapons that he uses in the world to distract and destroy the people that do their best in living for God. One of the best tactics that we must use as Christians is to follow orders given by our spiritual leaders. Just like in the military, when orders are given, all military positions pass them in the right order as protocol is observed. You cannot just fight on your own during war, you have to follow instructions given by your superiors. This is the same in spiritual life, we have to follow instructions that they give us, because our leaders are full of wisdom and knowledge that is necessary to equip us so that in the future, we will as well pass it to the next generation. God is the head of all principality and power, one thing we must know is that if we are in the army of God we are victorious. However, those who want to be successful will have to pass through various temptations and obstacles that are going to demand a lot of commitment and sacrifice, as a Christian you must be ready to fight the devices of the enemy then you shall reap a good harvest.

Introduction

The book of Genesis 1:1 tells us that in the beginning God created the heaven and the earth. The Bible goes on to teach us that it took God six days to create everything in existence today and He rested on the seventh day. On the sixth day, something special happened and that was when God created man in His own image. The first man was called Adam, later on God saw that Adam needed a companion and decided to put Adam in a deep sleep then He removed one of his ribs and created the first woman who was named Eve. They were both placed in the Garden of Eden.

Everything was good and wonderful in the Garden of Eden, God told Adam and Eve to eat everything there except the fruits borne by the tree of the knowledge of good and evil, God warned them that they would surely die if they ate the fruit of that tree. The book of Genesis 3:1 takes us to the serpent that was said to be subtler than any beast of the field which The Lord God had made. The serpent was the devil, he was cast away from heaven into the earth and he decided to make himself the god of the world. His first weapon to use against man was when he tricked Adam and Eve into eating the forbidden fruit that was in the Garden of Eden. He knew that doing that will harm God's relationship with men. After he tricked them into eating the forbidden fruit, immediately their eyes were opened and they could tell the difference between good and evil, they were even ashamed to face God after that incident.

The enemy was successful in his mission because his plan is to kill, steal and destroy just like the book of John 10:10 teaches; spiritual warzone began when the devil was cast out of the heaven into the earth. He was cast out with his team and the truth is that they are on earth today; it's a pity because we cannot see them with our eyes but we can see the damages that they are doing. This team of the devil is against the plans of God and their mission is to recruit as many people as they can before Judgement day comes which will send them to the lake of fire. The book of Revelation 21: 7 is a promise to us that He that overcomes shall inherit all things and God promises that He will be our God and we overcomers will become His children. This spiritual battle is real and dangerous. It is difficult to see that it exists because the pleasures of the world have blinded the minds of many people to think that life ends here on the earth. There is life after death, during death the soul only departs from the flesh which means that we have to start working on our personal walk with God right now whilst we are still on earth because that opportunity expires when death comes and there is no turning back.

Spiritual world war will always be there until the day God comes for judgement day. People tend to ignore this story, some people laugh at this story and they believe it is a fairy-tale, but it is not, the writer of this book Emmanuel N Tshuma experienced this spiritual world war ever since he was a kid and he continues to talk about it and he will until many people understand the impact of this war on earth today. We see two groups on battle on this war; the team of Satan (the devil) and the team of God. As individuals, we were given an opportunity by God to choose for ourselves which group we want to fall in, some have chosen to follow God whilst those who are still blinded by the pressures of this world are unaware that the devil knows they fall under his team, this shows how dangerous he is. He brings with him temporary happiness, joy and nice things that are only good for a certain period of time but causing eternal damage. On the other hand, it is difficult to live a life that is desired by God but the reward of that will be eternal joy and happiness which will last forever. The book of John 3:16 tells us that God sent His Son into the world to die for our sins, he who believes in Him shall not perish but have everlasting life. In this book we are going to have a how we can be successful in reaching Heaven as well as defeating the devil. We are also going to have a look at the weapons that the devil has placed in this world to discourage people and lead them into falling in his team.

We should be aware of the devil's weapons that he uses in this world and we should make sure that we are always alert at all times. God is looking for spiritual soldiers who are willing to fight and conquer the enemy. There are various spiritual leaders ready to mentor, teach and encourage all who are interested in joining the team of The Lord, great is their reward in Heaven.

Comparison of Spiritual and Military Leadership

The war we are living in a midst of, has been taking place since the devil was thrown out of Heaven, he knows that he has limited time and he is hunting day and night to seek someone that he can devour. The devil is the commander of darkness, he has spiritual weapons and armies that he uses on earth today, the good news is that God is the commander of the kingdom of Heaven, God is looking for men and woman on earth today who are ready to defend the truth, people who are ready to leave their sinful lives and work for God for the edification of His Kingdom. One of the most important areas that we must consider in the spiritual life is the area of leadership. The devil decided to move away from the orders that were given by his leader being God so he ended up destroying his reputation. People who do not follow what their leaders say never end up being successful, people who do not listen to what their bosses say end up in trouble. Soldiers who do not do orders given by their leaders end up in trouble as well as children who do not listen to what their parents say end up in trouble.

Leadership is therefore an important aspect of life and it is extra important in the spiritual life too. We have pastors today we have church leaders who are responsible for churches; they are there to show us the way. It is vital to follow what our leaders say, because they impart wisdom and knowledge to us that will in turn help us in the future to also teach others as well. In the spiritual there are various areas of leadership that are found and the positions can show a person which area they are located in the spiritual which will in turn help them to observe the importance of acknowledging and following leaders. It is the same in the military too, the positions are found below from our

Commander God until the last. We are going to have a look at them and begin elaborating them one by one. The positions are as follows:

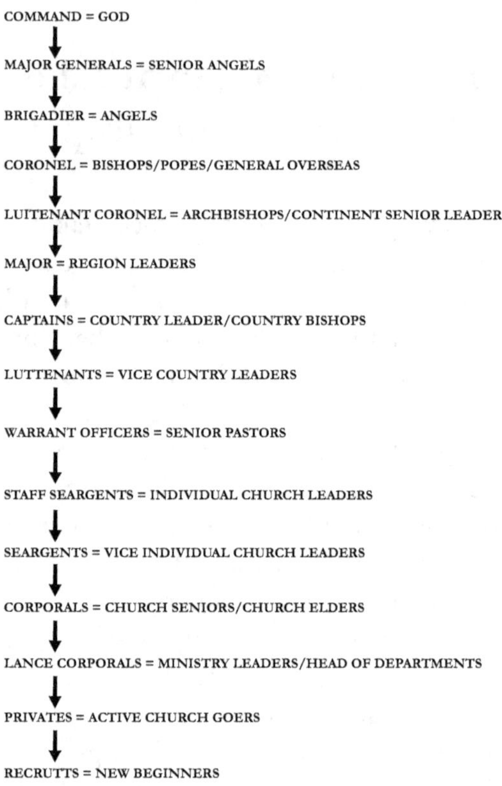

Commander=God

God is our Commander. He is our commander in chief. He created the Heavens and the earth just like the book of Genesis 1:1 tells us. Colossians 2:10 continues to tell us that God is the head of all principality and power. God was still the commander of the biblical battles that happened in the past. God was the commander of Moses and the Israelites in the Book of Exodus, He was there and through his power he helped them escape Egypt from Pharaoh. God was and will always be our Commander forever. We are His creation and we were made special. God has promised that one day He will come to take

His people to Heaven and those who will qualify to go to Heaven with Him will be those who would have been successful in working for His army, which is to obey His Word and live for Him.

People have different ways in which they call our Commander the everlasting God. Below are the sixteen names of God and what they mean:

Name	Meaning
El-Shaddai	Lord God Almighty
El-Elyon	The Most High God
Adonai	Lord, Master
Yahweh	Lord, Jehovah
Jehovah Nissi	The Lord My Banner
Jehovah Raah	The Lord My Shepherd
Jehovah Rapha	The Lord That Heals
Jehovah Shammah	The Lord Is There
Jehovah Tsidkenu	The Lord our Righteousness
Jehovah Mekoddishkem	The Lord Who Sanctifies You
El-Olam	The Everlasting God
Elohim	God
Qanna	Jealous
Jehovah Jireh	The Lord Will Provide
Jehovah Shalom	The Lord is Peace
Jehovah Sabaoth	The Lord of Hosts

(Insta encouragements, 2018)

God is the same yesterday, today and forever, The King of Kings and The Lord of Lords, He was there in the beginning all things were made by Him. He is the great Commander and chief in the Kingdom of Heaven, there is no one who is higher than Him. It is therefore a privilege to be a soldier in the army of God because it is already automatic that you are victorious.

Major Generals=Senior Angels

We have three senior angels found in the Bible. They are also recognized as archangels. Their names are St Michael, St Raphael and St Gabriel.

'Michael' means 'who is God?'; research indicates that He is one of the main angels. His name is a battle cry; both shield and weapon in the struggle against the enemy. We find St Michael in the book of Jude 1:9 which says 'But when the archangel Michael, contending with the devil, disputed about the body of Moses, he did not presume to pronounce a reviling judgment upon him, but said, "The Lord rebuke you".'

'Raphael' means 'divine healer'. He is a friend of the walkers and doctor of the sick, both physically and spiritually.

'Gabriel' means 'strength of God'. He had one of the most important missions: announcing to Virgin Mary that she would be the Mother of the Messiah. We find St Gabriel in the book of Daniel 9:21 where we see Daniel saying 'while I was speaking in prayer, the man Gabriel, whom I had seen in the vision at the first, came to me in swift flight at the time of the evening sacrifice'. (Churchpop, 2019)

Brigadiers=Angels

Zondervan Academic explains that angels are part of the universe that God created. The book of Nehemiah 9:6 goes on to say "Thou art the LORD, thou alone; thou hast made heaven, the heaven of heavens, with all their host, the earth and all that is on it, the seas and all that is in them; and thou preservest all of them; and the host of heaven worships thee". We see proof that angels were also created in this scripture. There are 3 types of angels which are:

Cherubim

- They guarded the entrance of the garden of Eden

- God is enthroned above them

- Two golden figures of cherubim sit above the Ark of the Covenant, where God promised to dwell among his people.

- They appear in the book of Exodus 25:20 which goes on to say 'And the cherubims shall stretch forth their wings on high, covering the mercy seat with their wings, and their faces shall look one to another; toward the mercy seat shall the faces of the cherubims be'.

Seraphim

- They appear in the book of Isaiah 6:2-7 which goes on to say 'above him stood the seraphim; each had six wings: with two he covered his face, and with two he covered his feet, and with two he flew'.

- They continually worshipping the Lord saying 'Holy. Holy, holy is The Lord of hosts; the whole earth is full of his glory'.

Living Creatures

- They appeared like a lion, ox, man or eagle representing various parts of God's creation, they too worship God continually

- Revelation 4: 8 goes on to say 'and the four living creatures, each of them with six wings, are full of eyes all round and within, and day and night they never cease to sing, "Holy, holy, holy, is the Lord God Almighty, who was and is and is to come!'

Angels have positions; there are high ranking angels such as St Michael who have power over other angels that is why they are referred to as archangels, and major generals on the military side. Angels often appear as messengers in the Bible and they are not omnipresent. The Bible does not specifically tell us how many angels exist but it seems they are a lot. Below are some of the points we should consider regarding angels:

- There are good angels and bad angels, the good belong to God and the bad ones belong to Satan.

- Angels do not marry

- Angels are not to be worshipped.

- Angels directly glorify God.

- Angels show us what perfect obedience looks like. (Grudem, 2017)

Colonels=Bishops/Popes/General Overseers

Bishops, popes and general overseers play a vital role in different kinds of churches existing today. Bishops have the right to lead every pastor in different branches across the world. They make sure that church things are carried out effectively and they also have the right to implement laws to be taken by other senior leaders across the world. Bishops are normally people who spent a lot of years in church, just like in the military, they are like colonels, they have a lot of experience in work and have so much wisdom and knowledge that is necessary to keep the church in general running through implementing, moulding, restoring and rebuking the leaders who are below them.

The Roman Catholic has what we call the pope. The pope is the general overseer of the whole church in general; even the big leaders listen to what he says because he is in a very important role in leadership that requires so much wisdom and impartation of The Word of God. General overseers are seen in most churches as well, these people are also above continental leaders, they are leaders who are in charge of all continents. Churches like The United Pentecostal Church have leaders in different kinds of leadership, for example, country leaders, region leaders, continental leaders and eventually general leaders. This kind of leadership is important because different powers are distributed to different leaders in order to avoid too many responsibilities that can end up straining an individual.

Different varieties like these are in relation to the military, this is what is called chain of commands. In the military when a person below is trying to report something, he first approaches the next chain of command above him until it eventually reaches the Commander, if the person decides to skip the chain of command normally the issue doesn't last and it can cause confusion, it is better to follow the chain of command first.

Luitenant Colonels=Archbishops/Continental Senior Leaders

Archbishops and continental senior leaders have the same positions like lieutenant colonels. They are responsible for different varieties of churches across continents all over the world. Their task is to give orders to the rest of the pastors in the whole continent. They are in charge of all decisions and new laws that are implemented in churches. Different types of churches existing today have these kinds of leaders in their communities.

Majors=Region Leaders/Missionaries

They are responsible for churches existing in regions of continents. They are normally referred to as region leaders or missionaries. For example in a region of SADC which is also referred to as Southern African Development Committee, it is a must for this region to have a leader who will be responsible for all countries located in the region. Churches like the United Pentecostal Church have these kinds of leaders and they normally travel around the countries visiting to check and see if things are done the right way.

Missionaries are pastors who are sent to minister in faraway places from their home with a motive of spreading the Word of God to places where it is difficult for people to get to know and understand what Christianity is all about. They started doing this wonderful job in the past since those days when Africa was colonised by the Europeans and other far away countries in the world. When the colonisation of Africa began, some did not go there to concentrate on colonising African states but they chose to goe and spread. The Word of God instead. Their mission was successful as we begin to see many African states having high numbers of Christians.

Missionaries continue doing this task even in the modern world as they continue travelling in countries preaching the Word of God, providing Bibles and other important materials. They also donate food and other necessities to the poor and the needy and they are also there to support churches. They play a very vital role in Churches and continue to move forward making sure that the Word of God is spoken and preached in different geographical areas in Africa as a whole and other parts of the world where people do not know about God.

Captains=Country Leaders/Country Bishops

Captains are leaders of all churches in a specific country. They are the ones who submit to the region leaders. They link the regional leaders with the vice country leaders of which we consider them as lieutenants. Their main roles are as follows:

- Making sure that all pastors in the country carry out the tasks that are assigned to them.

- Ordaining new apostles, prophets, evangelists, pastors and teachers.

- Responsible to invite new visitors who will be preaching or ministering in different churches across the country.

- Keeping a register of all church members, bible school learners and graduates, ministry leaders and pastors together with assistant pastors across the country as a whole.

- Responsible to suspend or appoint new pastors

- Making sure that pastors or church members who do not adhere to church standards are dealt with.

- Responsible to organise board meetings across the country.

Luitenants=Vice Country Leaders

Vice country leaders play a similar role with the captains who are regarded as country bishops. They support the country leaders in different variable ways such as follows:

- Making sure that he/she supports the country leader in each and every decision that is being made.

- Supporting and taking care of all church branches across the country when the country bishop is not around.

- Ensuring that all protocols are being followed where necessary.

- When the country bishop is held up or has travelled overseas for a certain period of time, the vice country leader does all duties of the country leader on his behalf.

Warrant Officers = Senior Pastors

Warrant officers are regarded to as senior pastors; they are pastors who have been leading church congregations for a long time, for example more than 10 years of their time as church members. They have so much experience in the church and they normally groom upcoming new pastors, teach, mould and give them knowledge on the tactics of forming a successful church.

These pastors are also Bible school directors. They are the backbone of the church and without them the church suffers. They also support the country bishop and the vice country leader.

When electing a country bishop or vice country leader, the senior pastors are the ones looked at as better candidates to fit the position for they have more wisdom and knowledge to teach and lead a congregation in general.

Staff Seargents = Individual Church Leaders

Individual church leaders are considered as one of the most important positions in Christianity. They are referred to as the leaders of the church congregations. This is where we find the five- fold ministry.

The Bible in Ephesians 4:11 says: And his gifts were that some should be apostles, some prophets, some evangelists, some pastors and teachers, (RSV). This five-fold ministry is found in the position of staff sergeants.

- **Apostles**: The Bible CD describes them as messengers or envoy. The term is applied to Jesus Christ, who was God's envoy to save the world, though, more commonly, the title is given to persons who were envoys commissioned by the Saviour himself.

- **Prophets**: A class of men of God, especially in the Old Testament dispensation, inspired to foretell future and secret events; and who also revealed the will of God as to current events and duties, and were his ambassadors to men. There are also prophets in this modern world who lead churches, they are also regarded as staff sergeants, individual church leaders and lead congregations. The most well-known prophets in this modern world include prophet T. B. Joshua, prophet Makandiwa, Major prophet Shepherd Bushiri just to mention a few.

- **Evangelists:** Evangelists play a very vital role in the ministry because they bring souls in the house of God. They are also church leaders; most of them own churches and the churches mostly have large numbers of people because of their great strength in soul winning and house to house follow-ups.

- **Pastors**: They are also known as Shepherds, whose office is to feed and guard the flock of Christ, pastors are owners of church congregations. Their role is to take care of the children of God. They are the backbone of the church.

- **Teachers**: Teachers play an important role in the ministry because of their wonderful ability to impart knowledge on people. They are the ones who groom upcoming apostles, pastors, evangelists, prophets and teachers as well. They are gifted in terms of teaching, delivering knowledge and also grooming.

Teachers are necessary and required in all churches, without them it is difficult to raise future ministers. They are normally involved in teaching ministries, Sunday school ministries and other discipleship classes. Teachers do a wonderful job as well in Bible school as they raise ministers of the gospel of God who are in the future going to win many souls for Christ which is in turn going to bring joy in Heaven.

Seargents= Vice Church Leaders

Vice church leaders are also known as assistant pastors. Their main role is to support the church leader when he or she is not around. They can be in the form of apostles, prophets, evangelists, pastors or teachers. Some basic roles that they play are as follows:

- They take care of the church when the church leader is not around.

- They support the church leader in each and every decision that is being carried out in the congregation.

- They make sure that other ministries or departments in the church are carried out in the right way.

- If at all there are issues that need to be dealt with, the vice church leaders can deal with them when the church leader is occupied or is far away. More complex issues are taken to the church leader by the vice if at all they have to be solved or dealt with.

- Vice church leaders are considered as sergeants also known as 2ICs of the church leaders. The word 2IC means vice, and this means in the absence of your leader you are the second in command.

Corporals=Church Seniors/Church Elders

Church seniors and church elders form a chain of command in the military known as corporals. They fall under the sergeant being the vice church leader and their role is to advice especially in the board. Without them the church feels empty because they have so much wisdom and knowledge that is necessary to equip all saints including the church leader and the vice. They are members who have been in the church for a long time exceeding 10 years. When the vice church leader or the church leader in general is selected, the board selects the members from the seniors, it is advisable because of their experience which is important for church growth. Other roles of the church seniors and elders are as follows:

- They can give advices to the church leader and the vice

- They are very good counsellors in whom where necessary they can counsel church members who are depressed, stressed or who seek for advices.

- When a family is not living in peace, church seniors have the ability to go and try to make peace through authorisation of the church leader.

- Church seniors have the ability to correct unwanted behaviour from church members who are not ready to adhere to church standards.

- When the church seniors or elders are not happy with anything in the church they can report directly to the church leader.

Lance Corporals=Ministry Leaders/Head of Departments

Ministry leaders are what we call, the body of the church. This is whereby we find different ministries working together forming one body, one body being the church which is the wife of Christ. The Bible speaks of a time when Jesus told one of his disciples named Simon Peter saying 'Upon this rock I shall build my church and the gates of hell shall not prevail against it'. Each ministry department has one member that is selected to take care of it. The ministry department normally has a vice in case the leader is held up to act as the temporary leader until the general leader is back. When the ministry department leaders are selected, they are selected from consistent church attenders who have been in church for a period of not shorter than 2 years and they have all the necessary requirements that are needed to be leaders. They are also required to have maturely grown and be able to visualize some spiritual things and also adhering to church standards. Let us take a look at the different departments found in churches of today:

- **Pulpit Ministry:** Most churches have what we call the pulpit. This is an area where someone stands to speak to the congregation. The church leader or pastor is the one in charge of this ministry, when he or she is absent, the vice church leader or the assistant pastor are in charge of this ministry. This is whereby they choose certain people to stand at the pulpit when addressing the congregation. Normally on each service, the Master of Ceremony also known as the (MC) leads the service, accompanied by the person who will be giving announcements, someone testifying, someone giving a word of encouragement and eventually the preacher who will be preaching on that day. The pulpit ministry is considered as one of the most sensitive and important ministries in the church. The church leader has to make sure that things are done in the correct order and manner because that is where visitors and the congregation get to see what the church is all about.

- **Praise and Worship ministry:** This ministry involves people who sing as well as those who play musical instruments. It is considered by some people as the first impression. Meaning that every person who visits church looks first at the church worship team. In the singing category, singers are normally classified as altos, sopranos, tuners and base. There are choirs as well in bigger churches with large numbers of people. This ministry requires someone with experience in music and singing so that he or she can in turn groom the upcoming youngsters and keep the generation moving.

- **Intercession ministry:** This ministry involves intercessors; these are saints who focus on prayer most of the time. Intercessors pray for the whole church and make sure that the church atmosphere is covered by the blood of Jesus Christ at all times. Some churches have intercessors that take turns and make sure that the church always has someone inside praying. This is considered as the number one step to answered prayers. In the Bible the book of 1 Thessalonians 5:17 directly tells us to pray without ceasing, intercessors play a very vital role in ensuring that this is being followed.

- **Ushering ministry**: This ministry involves those who stand at the entrance of the church to welcome visitors. This ministry is one of the most important because it makes the visitors feel welcomed in church so that they may come again in the next upcoming church services. Visitors who are not happy with the way they were treated in their first visit never bother to come back, so this ministry has to make sure that they give their best smile and make the visitors feel at home. Members of this ministry are called ushers. The other role of this ministry is to take tithes and offerings during services to maintain order as well as directing everyone who enters into the church showing them a place to sit.

- **Cleaning ministry**: This ministry ensures that the church is clean at all times. During days without services, members of this ministry come to church to clean and make sure that the church looks good.

- **Evangelism and follow up ministry**: This ministry consists of members who constantly check on all saints in the church and make sure that everyone is fine and well. Saints who are not feeling well emotionally, physically or spiritually are attended to by this ministry. They also go house to house preaching the Word of God and inviting people to come for services.

- **Men's ministry**: This ministry is for men. They are responsible to support the church in harder tasks that need manpower, for example when there are weddings, funerals, conferences, parties and other celebrations, men are responsible for fetching firewood, doing tasks like cooking meat, slaughtering animals and doing every other job that is required. This ministry is considered as one of the most important in church, without it the church suffers.

- **Women's ministry**: This ministry is for all women. It involves women coming together and supporting each other. Women normally support each other during baby showers and other events. They also play a very important task by ensuring that they help in weddings, funerals, conferences with cooking, preparing meals and decorating. This ministry is important in church because it gives a chance for all women to come together and work together in achieving the same goal.

- **Sunday school ministry**: This ministry involves young children, below the ages of 18. This is where children are taught The Bible. It is an area whereby the foundation of The Bible is laid on children's minds so that in the future, the teachings will not depart from their minds wherever they go. Studies indicate that children who started attending church whilst they were still young are not likely to leave church in the future.

- **Youth ministry**: This ministry involves adults who are 18- 35 years old. It is a ministry that is meant to revive the youth and also unite them together. This ministry normally establishes activities that help the youth to relate well with one another. Youth age is a tough stage in which most decisions come from, it is a stage that determines which life a person will live when he or she is old. Youth ministry makes sure that all youth in the church work together by counselling one another and supporting each other in good and hard times. Occasions such as youth conferences are very vital as they uplift the spiritual lives of the youth and help them create an atmosphere that brings them closer to God.

- **Teen ministry**: This ministry involves church members who are thirteen to nineteen years old. Its main purpose is to discuss issues that arise between the transitions of puberty stage to adult stage and to try to show guidance on how to tackle issues that need to be dealt with when approaching the adult stage. These teachings are important as they begin to build up the teens to be mature enough to face life in a different level when they are grown up.

- **Singles ministry**: This ministry involves adults who are single and not yet married, it differs with age and its main purpose is to join together all singles in church so that they discuss issues that affect them together with coming up with motives on how to tackle the situations.

- **Couple ministry**: This ministry is for married couples and its main aim is to come up with ideas on how to help each other as married couples. It creates an atmosphere to bond married couples as they discuss the issues they face and create solutions to them as a whole.

- **Nursery ministry**: It is a ministry that takes care of young babies under the age of 6 years, in order for a visitor or a member to worship and praise God freely in church, it is necessary for his or her baby to be taken to a safe room with someone who will be taking care of the baby until the service is over, the nursery ministry ensures that this is successfully carried out.

Privates=Church Attenders

Privates are considered as church attenders. These are people who know about God and they attend church on a daily basis. They are people who have accepted God and they have turned away from their old life and have passed through the new birth experience. Church attenders are classified into three main categories which are:

- **Senior class attenders**: They are church members who are active in church and attend church almost every week without fail. They actively participate in church activities and are always there when there is a need. Normally when a ministry leader is selected, the chances of a senior class attender being selected are very high.

- **Middle class attenders**: They are church members who do not attend church very frequently due to other related issues like work, travelling, or any other reason that is understandable. They do not just fail to come to church but situations force them to. Normally they are reliable because when they get a chance they do come to church without fail and they give their heart to God. Middle class attenders always support the church materially and financially although they do not attend church often. When there is a need at church, they come without fail if at all they are not held up at work.

- **Low class attenders**: These are members who come at church once in a while; they normally do not come often at church due to personal reasons. They do not actively participate in church activities and they do not actively support the church when there is a need. If they feel neglected they end up leaving church and go to attend elsewhere due to personal issues that might have hurt them in the past and the issues have not been dealt with.

Recruits/Trainees= Church Beginners

Church beginners are regarded as trainees. Church is the same as military life; the language that is spoken in Christianity is different from the language that is spoken in the world. The language that is spoken in the military is different from the language that is spoken in civilian life. It takes time to transform a civilian into military life just like it takes time to transform a person who does not know about God.

Church beginners are taken into different lessons when they want to fully be Christians. They are taught on how to be alert in the spiritual life, who God is, what the Bible is and why we have to be committed to God. One of the first lessons that are taught is the book of Genesis 1:1 which shows us how God created the heaven and the earth. We begin passing through the way God dealt with various people in the Bible from Adam and Eve passing through the lineages of Moses, Abraham, Ruth, Gideon, David until reaching the New Testament whereby we see Christ who died for our sins on the cross so that we will be saved. Church beginners are like a stage that is called military school in the army, a school whereby it converts a civilian into a well-qualified soldier with experience who is ready for war. The aim of church beginner conversion is for them to be able to be in the army of God that is ready to fight the spirits that are in this present world that we are living.

Spiritual Warzone

In the beginning of this book we had a look at how spiritual life is involved in Christianity, further relating military life to spiritual life as well as comparing military positions to physical positions.

The truth remains the same that we are living in a spiritual world as well, but we cannot see it with our own eyes. It takes someone with that spiritual ability to be able to feel and experience what really is happening. The fact is that there is a spiritual warzone taking place and that war will be fought until the day of the rapture and the second coming of Christ. Here is a story of what happened to one Christian by the name of Emmanuel N Tshuma living in Botswana.

On the year 2011, one dream occurred for Emmanuel and that dream changed the way he looked at things afterwards. On the year 2001, Emmanuel joined the church when he was only six years old; he stayed committed to church until the year 2006 when he fully decided to live for God. After the year 2006, things began to be tough for Emmanuel, his family moved from the place they were staying and this meant that he moved away from his friends and other close church members, to make things worse, Emmanuel got transferred from the Christian school called The Learning Centre School. This meant that he was to be taken to a government school which was different from the way he lived before. Time came, he got transferred and he started a new life, he had to make new friends, he had to adapt to the new environment, the way he prayed went down, the way he loved going to church slowly but surely changed. His Christian friends were rather far from him and that meant he had to fight on his own.

Things got worse and worse every year, life started becoming different, and on the year 2009 the young man went to secondary school to do form 1. There he met many people, peer pressure was high, Emmanuel began to see new things that he did not know but he chose to just be himself and strive to do what is right. That year was not that challenging like the year 2011, the year 2011 came so strong to Emmanuel such that he won't forget it for his entire lifetime. That was the year in which Emmanuel started to ask himself questions. It was a year in which he finished his junior school and was getting ready to go to senior school. He started thinking what life was all about, what made life fun, how to stop boredom (because he spent most of the time alone). Life was beginning to hold Emmanuel by the shoulder and he could see himself that something was missing and not right. Going often to church was a story of history, reading the Bible was something not common. Kneeling down, prayer and fasting were things of the past, Emmanuel was about to be thrown into the challenging eras of life when he had a dream that absolutely changed the way that he looked and analysed things.

It was a bright afternoon towards his junior certificate exams that were to be written. Those junior certificate exams determined if a student qualified to go to senior school or not. Many students boasted that after the day of the exams, they were free to do whatever they wanted because it was time for freedom. Those who wanted to fight had arranged to fight that day and Emmanuel was planning to launch some fights and arguments as well. Emmanuel that night had a strange dream. Whilst asleep Emmanuel saw something lifting him up on his bed, that thing looked like an angel of darkness but it looked obvious that it was not from God. It lifted Emmanuel and he could see his body remaining in bed whilst his soul and spirit were being taken away from his physical nature.

Emmanuel tried to fight but it was impossible the spirit was taking him further away from where he was sleeping and his home. He started crying for help but it was useless, that spirit was holding him tight such that he could not move away. After moments of struggle and fight with the spirit, Emmanuel remembered The Name of The Lord, suddenly he remembered that only Jesus could save him, he started calling on the name of The Lord and he shouted 'Jesus' Immediately that spirit began to shake and after a moment the spirit let him go and the spirit felt uncomfortable and ran away. Emmanuel returned successfully to his physical nature and he was back in bed. When he woke up it was in the middle of the night, Emmanuel realised that the dream was showing him something. Within a few days he interpreted the dream and he found out that the dream meant that he should be serious in the things of God or else the enemy (being the devil) and his team were waiting for him.

That month exactly after finishing writing his exams, Emmanuel went straight home after closing school and he cancelled those fights and arguments that he wanted to launch outside the school premises. When he got home, he received a call from one of his pastors that they were to attend an all-night of prayer at another church branch, Emmanuel straight away agreed and that night they went to the all night of prayer where Emmanuel received revival in his life after a long time and he decided to get back to his roots and be serious with God, he started praying, reading the Bible and becoming close to God, and never dreamt that strange dream ever again.

This is a true revelation that shows that there are many things that are happening in the spiritual world. We have to be alert of those things because if we are not careful, their mission is to destroy us and lead us to the pit of the enemy who knows that it will eventually lead to the burning fire in which the enemy and his team will be taken to during the second coming of The Lord.

There is spiritual warzone taking place, we encounter demons there, powers and principalities of the enemy, the rulers of the darkness of the world, spiritual wickedness in high places taking place, these spirits are in war with the team of angels of God but the good news is that the team of the devil knows that it has limited time left because it has already been defeated by God.

Key Scriptures

Below are the key scriptures that will be focused on the topic or subject of Spiritual Warzone. These scriptures talk about the way we are battling against spirits in this world.

- **Ephesians 6:12** for we are not contending against flesh and blood, but against the principalities, against the powers, against the world rulers of this present darkness, against the spiritual hosts of wickedness in the heavenly places. (RSV)

- **Colossians 1:9** and so, from the day we heard of it, we have not ceased to pray for you, asking that you may be filled with the knowledge of his will in all spiritual wisdom and understanding. (RSV)

- **Colossians 2:10** and you have come to fullness of life in him, who is the head of all rule and authority. (RSV)

- **Ephesians 1:21** far above all rule and authority and power and dominion, and above every name that is named, not only in this age but also in that which is to come. (RSV)

- **Philippians 2:10** that at the name of Jesus every knee should bow, in heaven and on earth and under the earth, (RSV

- **Matthew 28:18** And Jesus came and said to them, "All authority in heaven and on earth has been given to me. (RSV)

- **Colossians 2:15** He disarmed the principalities and powers and made a public example of them, triumphing over them in him. (RSV)

These scriptures give us a clue or an idea of what spiritual warzone is all about. As you look closely in these scriptures above you will realise that most of them talk about principalities and powers. These spirits battle against humans and they are being controlled by the devil. The good news as stated above is that God is the head of all principality and power just as mentioned in the book of Colossians.

2. In the book of Matthew 28:18, Jesus Christ clearly states that all authority in heaven and on earth has been given to Him. This means that the devil is already defeated, the lake of fire awaits him but he does not want to go alone, he wants to take many people with him.

How Spiritual Warzone Began

In the beginning God created the heaven and the earth (Genesis 1:1), on the sixth day, God created man. Man was then from since given authority to rule the earth. The book of Genesis 1:26 says 'And God said, Let us make man in our image, after our likeness: and let them have dominion over the fish of the sea and over the fowl of the air, and over the cattle, and over all the earth, and over every creeping thing that creepeth upon the earth'. So in other words man is living in flesh. The license to use when living on earth is flesh, there is no way you can live without flesh that is why God had to manifest himself into flesh in order to come on this earth to die for our sins. There is one important factor that we must understand on this earth, and this is spiritual power. Although we live on earth in the flesh, there are spiritual things happening around us, other spirits are right while other spirits are wrong. It is therefore important for us to be able to have an understanding of what is happening in the spirit. Let us take a look on how spiritual warzone began, and this story is found in the book of Revelation 12:7-12.

Revelation 12:7-12 And there was war in heaven: Michael and his angels fought against the dragon; and the dragon fought and his angels, 8 And prevailed not; neither was their place found any more in heaven. 9 And the great dragon was cast out, that old serpent, called the Devil, and Satan, which deceived the whole world: he was cast out into the earth, and his angels were cast out with him. 10 And I heard a loud voice saying in heaven, now is come salvation, and strength, and the kingdom of our God, and the power of his Christ: for the accuser of our brethren is cast down, which accused them before our God day and night. 11 And they overcame him by the blood of the Lamb and by the word of their testimony; and they loved not their lives unto the death. 12 therefore rejoice ye heavens, and ye that dwell in them. Woe to the inhabiters of the earth and of the sea! For the devil is come down unto you, having great wrath, because he knoweth that he hath but a short time.

The book of Revelation 12 tells us about war in Heaven, we are told that the devil and his angels were defeated, there was war in heaven.

After they were defeated they were cast on the earth. So the enemy is here on earth, he wants to defeat us humans, he does not want to go alone at hell, he wants to defeat humans on earth so that they are all cast on the lake of fire. The Bible tells us that Satan has been cast on earth with 1/3rd of the total number of angels in Heaven. That means 2/3rds of the angels are left on Heaven, 1/3rd of them are here on earth. So we must be careful of the enemy and his weapons. The enemy has camps where he stores his weapons to defeat humans; these are places which influence sin, these are places that involve things that are totally out of the will of God.

The Devil's Army

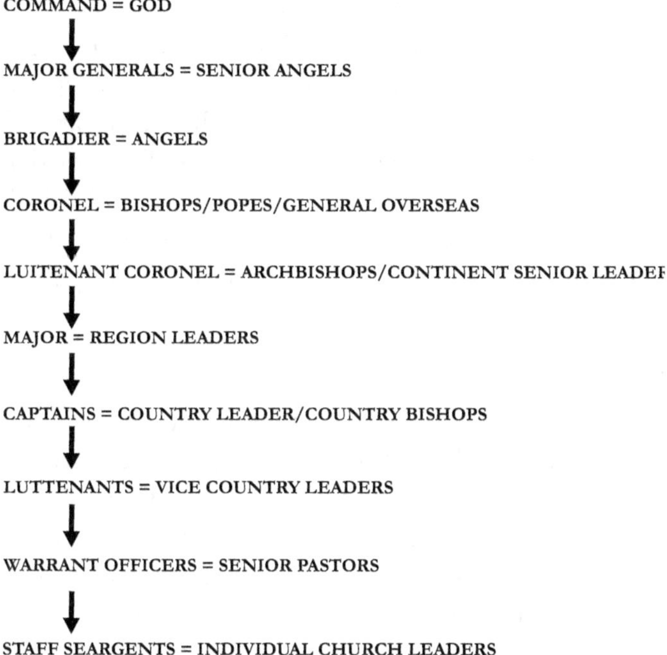

The Commander of the Opposition Team (Satan)

The enemy himself (the devil) has made himself the god of this world. He considers himself as the commander of this world. His time is limited, he is already defeated in hell but unfortunately he does not want to go alone, he wants to take someone with him. After he was cast into the earth, he came to earth whereby we learn in the book of Genesis of how he tempted Eve to eat the forbidden fruit that they were instructed by God not to eat. Due to his cleverness the enemy succeeded in tricking Eve to eat the forbidden fruit who also gave it to Adam. The consequences of their actions were hurting and painful. They were removed out of the Garden of Eden and life changed afterwards. As a punishment, man was forced to do hard labour, to sweat in order to provide to the family, the woman was to carry a child in her womb for nine months and as well go through labour pains during delivery.

The danger part of sin is that in the beginning, it looks so good but at the end the results are painful and hurtful, this is the tactic that the enemy uses to convince people that sin is good and there is nothing wrong with it. In the table above we see the devil's army, he is the commander of the dark kingdom and he has different departments under him which are the rulers of the darkness of the world, evil powers, principalities and lastly Satanism, Let us quickly browse through them before getting into the weapons used by the enemy un this world.

The Nature of Sin

This falls under the devil's army, it deals with the activities that are taking place in this world that we are living in. There are many rulers who seem to be eager in controlling the world. One of the factors is sin; the definition of sin means to turn away from God. When a person sins, God turns away from them. The book of Isaiah 59:2 clearly states that (Isaiah 59:2 but your iniquities have separated between you and your God, and your sins have hid his face from you, so that he will not hear). The enemy uses sin to distract Christians from God. He knows that sin is easy to do but hard to stop, many people fall on this trap each and every day, we are living in a world that is very tough and tempting, it takes a very committed person to avoid sin at all costs and live a life that is meaningful and wanted by The Lord. The Bible in the book of John chapter three verses sixteen explains to us of how Jesus Christ died on the cross for our sins so that we could have eternal life; it is time for Christians to be alert on the devices of the enemy and live acceptable lives wanted by God. Let us take a look at some few verses that talk about sin.

Job 15:16 How much more abominable and filthy is man, which drinketh iniquity like water?

Proverbs 11:3 the integrity of the upright shall guide them: but the perverseness of transgressors shall destroy them.

Hosea 5:6 they shall go with their flocks and with their herds to seek the LORD; but they shall not find him; he hath withdrawn himself from them.

Luke 11:4 and forgive us our sins; for we also forgive every one that is indebted to us. And lead us not into temptation; but deliver us from evil.

Romans 12:21 be not overcome of evil, but overcome evil with good.

The Bible clearly shows us how sin is bad and dangerous therefore we must avoid it at all costs. Sin is of the devil and he uses it to destroy many people including Christians in the world. When we sin, we leave the throne of God and move into the throne of the devil. It is even difficult for an individual who has sinned to even go to church or pray during a specific time because they will be having that guilt inside of them that will be criticizing them of how they are not perfect before The Lord. At certain times sin can even make an individual at church loose his/her concentration because they will start judging themselves as sinners, this is how dangerous sin can be. We have to be strong and alert always, this is doing our best in living a life desired by The Lord.

The Lord promises us in the book of Acts 2:38 that if we repent, He shall wipe away our sins and make us new, if at all you have sinned and you are worried on how God will look at you , be encouraged by the book of Acts 2:38. The book of Romans 3:23 tells us that all have sinned and come short of the glory of God. The book of Romans 6:23 continues teaching us that the wages of sin is death but the gift of God is eternal life. We need the grace of God always and we need to repent our sins every day. There is np repentance after death and there is no repentance during judgement day. Make it a priority to fix and activate your spiritual life whilst you are still living on earth because life is too short. You may never know what will happen tomorrow.

Evil Powers

According to (Your Dictionary), it defines evil as a quality of being morally bad or something that causes harm or misfortune, or destruction. Being evil can also be categorized as witchcraft, this refers to a practice of magical skills, spells and abilities. Some people define witchcraft as the work of crones who meet secretly at night, indulging in cannibalism and orgiastic rites with the devil. Black magic is also associated with witchcraft. One man by the name of Jeffrey Burton Russell says that witchcraft is derived from the old English word wiccecraeft from wicca (masculine) or wicce(feminine) pronounced 'witchah' denoting someone who practices sorcery; and from craeft meaning (craft) or 'skill'.

Evil powers and witchcraft fall under the category of the devil as well and people on earth must be careful with whom they deal with and what they do as well as where they go. It is difficult to signify or see a witch in this present world because the work takes place in secret but it is real. People must be careful in everything that they do and the medicine to kill witchcraft is only one and that is prayer, asking The Lord for His intervention because He is the head of all principality and power.

Principalities

The enemy operates under principalities as well; these principalities are plans of the devil to destroy the world and his team. Their mission is to lead as many people as they can to hell before judgement day comes. Demons and other contrary spirits are in existence even in this present world. Demons fall under the study of demonology. Demonology is the study of Satan and other contrary spirits and demons, they are spirits that can possess someone, when someone is possessed, he or she needs to be delivered from that spirit, churches have different ways in casting out those spirits, some churches do a process called deliverance whereby they pray for that particular person for the demon to come out, other churches do certain different rituals that are believed to destroy the spirit.

Deliverance from the spirits of the devil is found in The Bible; Luke 11:4 says 'And forgive us our sins; for we ourselves also forgive every one that is indebted to us. And bring us not into temptation'. Our wish as Christians is for us to ask The Lord to deliver us from all forms of evil because they are real and tormenting. We should be strong enough to resist the plans of the enemy so that our walk with God as Christians will not be affected.

Satanism (History.com Editors, 2019)

Satanism falls under the category of the devil, it is more like a religion which is practiced in secret but slowly beginning to be recognized in the world. It is a group of ideological and philosophical beliefs based on Satan. Studies indicate that the official satanic church was formed by Anton LaVey. Satanism did not exist as a real organized religion but was commonly claimed as real by Christian churches. These claims surfaced particularly when persecuting other religious groups. It has been told that sometime between 1957 and 1960, Antony Lavey, a former carnival worker and musician used to hold night classes which eventually formed the church of Satan. The meetings were ritual based and other certain rituals which ended up giving Lavey the name of the black pope. Studies further indicate that the Satanic church early recruiting efforts included the short-lived Topless Witches Revue nightclub show, the Satanic Bible was also published in 1969 which brought together Lavey's personal mix of black magic and occult concepts, the Satanic Bible served as a strong material for the growth of the church of Satan.

As the Church of Satan grew in number, some members decided to split and they went to form their own branches, some of the churches include The First Occultic Church of Man in 1971 formed by Wayne West, and The Temple of Set in 1975 formed by Newsletter editor Michael Aquino. The most successful result of church divisions is the satanic temple, it first gained attention in 2013, the temple was recognized as a religion by the US government in 2019, and has grown to include about 20 temples across North America.

Satanism is true and existing in this world we are living in, people are actually being delivered from Satanism in churches, normally the deliverance sessions take longer than ordinary ones because Satanism is a deep spiritual group that is more harmful, some studies indicate that the sacrifices that are practiced there are very scary as well as the way blood is involved.

Satanism is the reverse of Christianity. Satanists worship Satan, Christians worship God. The greatest enemy of Christians is Satan, whilst Satanists consider their greatest enemy to be God. The true story is that God is, more powerful than anything else in this universe, meaning He is the head of heaven and earth, the starts and moons together with the nine planets of the solar system Mercury, Venus , Earth, Mars, Jupiter, Saturn, Uranus, Neptune and Pluto. The book of Colossians 2:10 says 'and in him ye are made full, who is the head of all principality and power': God is the commander of everything. Nothing is impossible for Him. He can do miracles and wonders to those who put their trust in Him

Weapons used by the Devil in the World

The truth will remain the same and the fact is that the devil is in existence in earth today, he has been there since creation. A spirit that is unseen but causing great damage on the physical. Let us have a look on the weapons that the enemy uses in the world in the below table then we will broaden them up after the table whereby we will be dealing with each point. These weapons have been classified as physical and spiritual.

Physical Weapons used by the Enemy

Diseases/ Illnesses	Corruption	Revenge
World War	Inequality	Love of Money
Technology	Discrimination	Abuse
Arguments	Miserable lives	Stealing
Pride of life	Sexual immorality	Unplanned events

Spiritual Weapons Used By The Enemy

Deadly Commited By Mouth Sins The Unwanted Commited In Areas Acts Various

Lying	Anger
Gossiping	Laziness
Slander	Discontentment
Tale-bearing	Lust
Sowing discord	Depression
Cursing	Jealousy
Filthy language	Hatred
Blasphemy	Un-forgiveness
Contentious speech	Backsliding
Unbelief	Selfishness

Examining The Physical Weapons Used By The Enemy In The World

A. Diseases/Illnesses

Diseases and illnesses are one of the world leading areas where people lose their lives. The enemy uses diseases to distract people from God. It is difficult for an individual to pray well when they are sick or even attend a church service, that on its own affects the spiritual life on an individual. We are living in a world whereby there are many illnesses; these diseases are classified in classes such as:

Congenital	kidney diseases	Respiratory illnesses	Eye illnesses	Metabolic	Vitamin related
Endocrine and genetic disorder	Mental illnesses	Skin diseases	Gastrointestinal	Physical	Blood related
Fungal	Neurological	Viral and communicable	Human Syndromes	Sexual	Parasitic
Heart diseases	Pregnancy associated	Dental illnesses	Lung illnesses	Stomach illnesses	Cancer

Diseases have affected the world at a very high rate and they are costly as well, the affect the world physically, mentally, financially and spiritually as well. One of the world's leading diseases includes Cancer, HIV and AIDS, and Covid19. These viruses have caused more deaths in the world more than any illnesses. The world's most dangerous, being Covid19 has led to more than one million deaths in less than two years since its discovery on December 2019. Covid19 has greatly affected the economy, many businesses are operating at a loss, some have closed permanently and some will never open again. Many families have lost their loved ones. These illnesses are associated with the spirits of the enemy which are meant to kill, steal and destroy just like the book of John 10:10 says.

It is time for people to seek The Lord, God is the way, the truth and the life, those who put their trust on Him shall never lack. The

Book of Matthew 10 verse 1 tells us of a time when Jesus Christ called forth the twelve apostles, the Bible says He gave them power to heal all manner of sickness and diseases. We are the chosen apostles of today; we have been given power to pray for each other so that God may heal everyone who is sick. We just need to seek the face of The Lord just like the book of Matthew 6:33 tell us then we shall see The Lord doing great and mighty things on our lives.

Sicknesses and diseases should not control us in this world but we must have the strength to control them so that they may not prevail against us, in order to win this battle we must ask the Creator of the heaven and the earth to help us fight this weapon because it is very dangerous for it has caused many challenges and situations that are beyond control and have left many hopeless. The only solution is prayer.

B. Worldwar

World war is one of the weapons that the enemy uses to destroy Christians. World wars cause people never to be free, people are always fearful for the safety of their lives, peace and harmony is never found and many people have lost their lives during world wars. The greatest wars that have ever happened in human history are World War I and World War II.

Studies indicate that World War I also known as the First World War or the Great War was centred in Europe. It began on 28 July 1914 until it ended on 11 November 1918. More than 9 million combatants and 7 million civilians died as a result of the war. It was one of the deadliest conflicts in history, paving the way or causing major political changes. More than 70 million military personnel, including 60 million Europeans were mobilised in one of the largest wars in history.

Studies also indicate that World War II also known as the Second World War was a global war that lasted from 1939 to 1945, though related conflicts began earlier. It involved a vast majority of the world's nations, including all of the great powers, eventually forming two opposing military alliances: the Allies and the Axis. It was the most widespread war in history, and directly involved more than 100 million people from over 30 countries, the major participants threw the entire economic, industrial, and scientific capabilities behind the war effort. It resulted in an estimated 50 million to 85 million fatalities making World War II the deadliest conflict in human history. (History of The World, 2016)

During these world war times it meant that churches were not operating, it affected activities like evangelism and other important church activities, in short it was destruction by the enemy to enable people to be afraid for the safety of their lives and stay home. It was even difficult to convert a person to Christianity because of the destructions that were taking place every day, people lost hope and people died painful deaths, others died innocently and it was pain and suffering everywhere. This weapon was the greatest ever weapon used by the enemy to cause destruction in the world, our wish as people in the world currently is to avoid any further world wars taking place, we have had enough and it is now time to practice peace and harmony in all countries in the world. Issues must be solved in a proper way without violence or else it will be a gateway for the enemy to cause havoc and cause unnecessary wars.

C. Technology

In the olden days when technology was still low, people were not much into it, because only a few could afford the latest inventions. But as time went on over the centuries and decades, people slowly got into technology until most of the people in the present life own latest technology items, below are some of the well-known technologies:

- Televisions, Cell phones, computers and play station

- Social media (Facebook, WhatsApp, Snapchat, Instagram etc.).

- Cars, buses, trains and airplanes.

- The Internet (Google etc.)

Technology has become the source of everything in human life, it has replaced many things that were done in the past, one of the examples includes creation of jobs, due to more modified machines, the use of human labour has been reduced thus killing many jobs that would have done by human beings, the lack of jobs creates stress and worry to most people who end up living unsatisfied lives that are going to make them disagree that God really exists, they ask themselves questions such as 'If God is indeed living why is my life like this'.

Other technologies such as phones, laptops and television have taken most of the time and people have reduced the way they fellowship at home, at school at work because their concentration is always on these devices, that damages unity and cooperation and the enemy likes a place that has no unity because he knows people will not work together to achieve common goals but instead, people will criticise one another and cause further problems.

We must rise up as people and understand these things, we must understand that technology helps us but let us be alert on it never let it destroy our lives spiritually because it damages our relationship with God, and when our relationship with God is low it will be difficult for Him to help us.

D. Arguments

Emmanuel N Tshuma defines an argument as a situation in which two or more people do not agree on a certain issue or when an either party challenges a motion set up by the other. Disagreements are found everywhere and the truth is they cannot be avoided. In a place where people are there will always be some who do not agree to a certain provided topic. The enemy uses arguments to separate people and destroy an understanding for each other; arguments contribute to other factors such as criticism, anger, wrath, fighting just to mention a few. When people are in argument, they should be mature enough to control the way they talk to each other or else they end up creating a havoc which becomes more dangerous. Let us have a look at different scenarios in which arguments are created and how they can be controlled in time:

- Arguments at home: These are arguments that happen at home. They can either be husband and wife, wife and child, husband or child or either on relatives on the house. There will be always time whereby there are certain things that are being disagreed on a family but people must learn to respect what the authority says, the husband is the head of the house, just like God being the commander of the heaven and the earth. At the end of the day members of the family must accept what the head says even though they dislike what is being said. The head must also respect what the other members say and listen attentively to what they say without crushing them; things must be done in a proper way without hate, anger and favouritism.

- Arguments at work: At a workplace there will be always be disagreements, in most issues , employees do not feel comfortable with the decisions done by their employers but they must learn to accept and move on working.

- Arguments at church: Most of the churches have what we call the board. These are members who are responsible for most activities done at church, they normally have disagreements as well but they must learn to accept one another and listen to the pastor or church leader.

- Arguments in politics: There are always arguments taking place in politics, members normally disagree on many issues on a daily basis, but in order for a political party to win, they have to be united and on one mission with the party president. Political parties who disagree with each other stand at a low chance of winning elections.

The fact will remain the same that arguments will always lead to failure. No argumentative group, school, business or family has ever succeeded because they are not on the same mission, the enemy loves situations like these because he knows that people like that won't go anywhere in life. We have to embarrass the enemy by agreeing with each other on meetings and working together to achieve a common goal. We must never allow arguments to control our lives because at the end we become the ones who lose the battle, we are fighting against principalities and powers, arguments are one of those principalities that have to be defeated by the blood of Jesus Christ.

The Bible also warns us of arguments, the book of 2 Corinthians 12:20 which says 'For I fear, lest by any means, when I come, I should find you not such as I would, and should myself be found of you such as ye would not; lest by any means there should be strife, jealousy, wraths, factions, backbiting's, whisperings, swellings, tumults;' all these things can be caused by arguments, let us control arguments at all costs.

Epride of Life

The English dictionary defines pride as feeling excessively, the act and habit of arrogating, or making undue claims in an overbearing manner; that species of pride which consists in exorbitant claims of rank, dignity, estimation, or power, or which exalts the worth of importance of the person to an undue degree. It can also mean proud contempt of others; lordliness; haughtiness; self-assumption; presumption.

Pride is one of the weapons that the enemy uses to defeat Christians; it is also one of his top three favourite weapons, which are the lust of the flesh, the lust of the eyes and the pride of life. Let us have a look on a couple of verses in The Bible that talk about pride:

1John 2:16 For all that is in the world, the lust of the flesh and the lust of the eyes and the vain glory of life, is not of the Father, but is of the world.

Luke 16:15 and he said unto them, Ye are they that justify yourselves in the sight of men; but God knoweth your hearts: for that which is exalted among men is an abomination in the sight of God.

Obadiah 1:4 Though thou mount on high as the eagle, and though thy nest be set among the stars, I will bring thee down from thence, saith Jehovah.

Proverbs 28:25 He that is of a greedy spirit stirreth up strife; but he that putteth his trust in Jehovah shall be made fat.

The Bible condemns pride as well because pride cannot take someone somewhere, when an individual views themselves better than others, at the end of the day they accomplish nothing at all. Many men have fallen who were once prideful in life, they boasted and saw themselves better than others, they mocked , criticized and made fun of others but one day life changed and it put them down and they became more hurt than before. The Book of Obadiah explains to us that even if we consider ourselves better, God can put us down at any time because He has the power and ability to do so.

May the good Lord help us to avoid being prideful, those who are not prideful live happy lives because The Lord blesses such greatly. If you are an individual and you deserve to life a long happy life, avoid pride by all means. Even when The Lord blesses you greatly and mightily, avoid boasting about it and keep it in secret, avoid telling everyone about your success because not everyone will like it and that's when jealousy begins which can create further problems. People have a tendency of posting their success on social media especially Facebook and WhatsApp, that is risky because you might never know what people are planning you, it is better you keep your success to yourself so that The Lord can take you higher and higher until success itself starts following you wherever you go. Let us say a big NO to pride.

F. Corruption

Google defines corruption as dishonest or fraudulent conduct by those in power, typically involving bribery. Corruption hinders the development of the economy, it wastes the state's resources and affects local and foreign investments due to lack of incentives.

The Bible also talks about corruption, it does not only affect the economy but it affects spirituality as well. Below are a couple of verses that talk about corruption:

Psalms 12:1 [To the chief Musician upon Sheminith, A Psalm of David] Help, LORD; for the godly man ceaseth; for the faithful fail from among the children of men.

Isaiah 59:3 for your hands are defiled with blood, and your fingers with iniquity; your lips have spoken lies, your tongue hath muttered perverseness.

Ezekiel 43:8 in their setting of their threshold by my thresholds, and their post by my posts, and the wall between me and them, they have even defiled my holy name by their abominations that they have committed: wherefore I have consumed them in mine anger.

Matthew 6:13 And lead us not into temptation, but deliver us from evil: For thine is the kingdom, and the power, and the glory, for ever. Amen.

Romans 8:21 because the creature itself also shall be delivered from the bondage of corruption into the glorious liberty of the children of God.

1 Corinthians 15:53 for this corruptible must put on incorruption, and this mortal must put on immortality.

There are a lot of verses found in the Bible that oppose corruption, because even in the spiritual it destroys, it destroys honesty and faithfulness and makes an individual impure. People must understand that things done in favour can ruin further in the future, a typical example can be when a church leader chooses or nominates a head of a ministry who is not fit but due to the fact that he or she impresses the church leader maybe in participating in church activities, the leader ends up choosing him/her, it is going to affect that particular ministry that will hinder it from growing to the desired standard.

Below are some of the factors that will help us avoid corruption at home, school, and church and at the workplace

- Being honest at all times and avoiding hiding the truth, although sometimes it can be hard or even make an individual being hated for saying what is right.

- Making the truth, our first priority, there is a saying which says 'tell the truth and it will set you free'. The good part of saying the truth is that , in the future that certain scenario will not affect an individual psychologically but rather it will create a free mind, the bad part of saying a lie and keeping things in the heart without saying them out is that they will haunt the particular individual for the rest of their lives.

- Avoiding bribery , this involves giving or receiving something from someone with the intention of obtaining favour from them without the knowledge of others.

G. Inequality

Inequality refers to the state of being unjust; others define it as a state of being unfair. There are many instances in which we find inequality being done. We come across situations in which people are treated unequally. When people are not treated fairly, this creates hatred, jealousy and several other instances that are not good at all. A typical example is at the workplace, when the manager decides to call on a party or braai and he/she invites other workers in his/her company instead of inviting all workers we call that inequality. When a church leader decides to share some important/relevant information to some of his board members instead of telling all board members we call that inequality. Instances as such break the unity and bond especially in church leading to situations that are not pleasing or satisfying. Let us take a look on a couple of verses in the Bible that talk about inequality:

Proverbs 31:31 Give her of the fruit of her hands; and let her own works praise her in the gates.

Ezekiel 18:25 yet ye say, The way of the Lord is not equal. Hear now, O house of Israel; Is not my way equal? are not your ways unequal?

Romans 9:21 Hath not the potter power over the clay, of the same lump to make one vessel unto honour, and another unto dishonour?

Colossians 4:1 Masters, give unto your servants that which is just and equal; knowing that ye also have a Master in heaven.

The Lord encourages us to be practice equality amongst one another on earth, when we carry out inequality on others, this creates space for the enemy to hop in and destroy, inequality is one of the secret weapons used by the enemy on earth because inequality happens slowly but showily causing little damage until time comes when it is very difficult to bring things back to normal again. At times people do not understand the difference between equality and leadership, there are several times in which people think they are treated unequal by their leaders, but the truth is not everyone has the same ability, sometimes the reason why leaders choose specific people to do certain tasks different from others is because those specific people could be fit to do the task. The greatest factor to consider as a leader is to be mature enough to weigh circumstances and issues by making sure that his/her people are treated equally and just.

One novel by the name of Animal farm, talks about an area of equality whereby animals felt that humans treated them unequal but soon after they fired humans in their farm they came to realise that some animals are more equal than others because there will be no time in planet earth whereby people's capabilities are the same. There will be always others who are more gifted than others no matter what, the only option is to accept each other and work together in achieving one common goal, and this is never giving the devil a chance to interfere in the areas where we feel inequality is appropriate. May God give us the ability to be just and fair with one another.

H. Discrimination

Discrimination refers to the state of unacceptance to a certain group of people because of their skin colour, tribe, ethnic group or race. We discover many instances in world in which discrimination is being practiced. There are ethnic groups existing in the world that discriminate each other, country nationals discriminate each other, groups of people discriminate each other, others even get to a point of killing each other just because of discrimination. The truth is there is unhappiness in discrimination, this causes pain and where there is pain, the enemy is always involved, the enemy does not want to see people happy, when he sees them he will think of alternative plans to destroy that happiness, the enemy enjoys instances in which people are unhappy. Below are a couple of verses in The Bible that talk about discrimination:

Leviticus 10:10 And that ye may put difference between holy and unholy, and between unclean and clean;

Proverbs 17:15 He that justifieth the wicked, and he that condemneth the just, even they both are abomination to the LORD.

Hebrews 5:14 But strong meat belongeth to them that are of full age, even those who by reason of use have their senses exercised to discern both good and evil. {of full age: or, perfect} {use: or, an habit, or, perfection}

The Bible condemns discrimination; there are instances in the church today in which members discriminate each other. A typical example is when one of the church members commits a sin that becomes well known to most of the church members, they begin to avoid that particular individual and see themselves more better than him, the fact will remain the same that all have sinned just like the book of Romans 3:23 says. Only God has the power and ability to judge, we have no right to judge others by their faults but we have the right to correct them and show them the right way that God wants us to live on this earth.

The danger part of discrimination in the church is that when a particular individual feels neglected just because people do not want to fellowship with him or her, that particular person may end up leaving church, and now we come back to the mission of the enemy which is to remove Christians from Christ and take them to the road that leads to the lake of fire, we must unite together and fight discrimination. It does not affect spiritual issues but it also affects the economy at large, an economy that discriminates is never successful.

Discrimination is one of the weapons that we need to be careful about in this present life, if not treated well in time it can cause more harm therefore it has to be avoided at all costs, many people have lost their lives due to discrimination this has led to pain and hurt to their families, we will not go anywhere in life when we discriminate each other, we were created by God in His image therefore we must appreciate God's creation by living in harmony with one another without judging and neglecting others.

I. Miserable Lives

There are people who live miserable lives in this world that we live in, people may not be happy due to different circumstances. Living miserably has certain attributes that are not pleasing towards the end for example stress, anxiety, loneliness and depression, living miserably is also not good for our health. When a person is living a miserable life, it is difficult for them to trust that God will intervene in their situation. This ends up creating an opportunity for the enemy to get involved and use that as an obstacle for them to give up on trusting on God. There are different scenarios in which we see miserable lives happening, typical examples are below:

- At work: A person may live miserably at work due to other co-workers mistreating him/her even the manager/boss. That particular individual must bear in mind that he/she has come to work so that he/she makes money to support the needs and wants not a community/people to impress.

- At school: At some instances, a student may feel mistreated by his/her classmates, schoolmates or even teachers, this tends to affect the particular individuals even in their studies, this may being stress and unhappiness, the best way is for that particular individual to report the matter to his/her parents or even the head teacher if at all one of the teachers makes his/her life miserably.

- At home: Most of people who live miserable lives are seen at home, this may be if at all there were disagreements in the family that led to that or disputes and misunderstandings, these issues must be dealt with as early as possible, people must seek for counselling from pastors, trusted friends or the community at large, there is no point in living miserably whilst you can seek for help.

Most of the issues in the world of people living miserably are their background, people have a tendency of thinking that since they came from a poor background that means God has forgotten about them but the truth is life is never fair. It is not your fault when you are born poor but it becomes your fault when you die poor, God has given us many abilities and time so that we may make something and live better lives, we should rise up, trusting in God and prayer and say NO in leaving ,miserable lives. The Lord will help those in need at every minute and second if you seek Him. The book of Matthew 6:33 tells us that if we seek Him first He shall provide us what we need , if we live miserable lives He will turn our unhappy lives into happy lives.

J. Sexual Immorality

Sexual immorality is defined as a situation in which people are involved in sexual encounters that are not pleasing to God and The Bible strictly condemns them. There are various areas of sexual immorality that are taking place in this world that we are living in, the enemy uses this weapon to destroy Christians, his main target is on sexual immorality. Out of the top three missions that the enemy has targeted on the world, sexual immorality is involved because the lust of the eyes and the lust of the flesh that leads to that. Sexual immorality should be avoided at all costs because it destroys many Christians that will have gone far in the spiritual and brought revival to the lost souls in the world, being involved in sexual immorality makes a Christian feel that they are no longer fit to continue being serious in the things of God because they see themselves as unfit to do so, the enemy brings guilt in them. Below are typical examples of sexual immorality and what the Bible says about them:

- *Fornication: This is engaging in sexual intimacy before marriage. The book of 1Corinthians 6:13 says 'Meats for the belly, and the belly for meats:* but God shall destroy both it and them. Now the body is not for fornication, but for the Lord; and the Lord for the body.' Fornication must be avoided.

- *Adultery:* This refers to engaging in sexual intimacy with someone who is married. This has led to many cases of divorce around the world and it should be avoided at all costs. The book of Exodus 20:17 says 'Thou shalt not covet thy neighbour's house, thou shalt not covet thy neighbour's wife, or his manservant, or his maidservant, or his ox, or his ass, or anything that is thy neighbour's'. The Bible strictly condemns adultery because it is very dangerous, the enemy is interested in using weapons as such to destroy marriages, it is time to disappoint the enemy and be faithful to one another.

- *Incest:* This is sexual intimacy with a close relative or family member, it is strictly prohibited

- *Same-sex encounters:* This is sexual intimacy with the person of the same sex, it is strictly prohibited by the Bible

- *Pornography:* This is the viewing of sexual material on the internet or through televisions, phones or any other device; it is one of the dangerous because it contributes to all areas of sexual immorality.

Sexual immorality can be avoided, the greatest challenge that people face nowadays is that sexual material is accessible at any time at any area giving an atmosphere for people to view it, the good news is that it can be avoided through prayer, asking the Lord's intervention and confessing to God will help as well as changing the way of life being lived, this is whereby hobbies, games, reading books and music are done instead of spending time thinking about sexual immorality. May God open up our eyes so that we can do what is right and be an inspiration to the upcoming generation that will be able to find us with wisdom and knowledge.

K. Revenge

Revenge refers to using, treating or giving someone or something the same way it was done to you. Most people love to revenge, they want to treat others the way they were treated badly, little do they know that that does not make them any better, we need to learn to stop revenging because it is not right. The enemy loves people who revenge because they are normally full of anger, pride and hate which makes the enemy even happier, thus making revenge a dangerous weapon used by the devil. Let us look at a couple of verses before that talk about revenge:

Deuteronomy 32:41 If I whet my glittering sword, and mine hand take hold on judgment; I will render vengeance to mine enemies, and will reward them that hate me.

Proverbs 20:22 Say not thou, I will recompense evil; but wait on the LORD, and he shall save thee.

Romans 13:4 for he is the minister of God to thee for good. But if thou do that which is evil, be afraid; for he beareth not the sword in vain: for he is the minister of God, a revenger to execute wrath upon him that doeth evil.

Matthew 5:39 But I say unto you, That ye resist not evil: but whosoever shall smite thee on thy right cheek, turn to him the other also.s

The Bible itself condemns revenge, the book of Romans 13:4 tells us that The Lord will execute wrath to those who do evil, if someone does something to us, The Lord will punish them. The book of Matthew 5:39 explains to us as well that if anyone slaps you on your right cheek, you should give them your left cheek so that they slap at you without revenging. This may seem foolish but the fact remains the same that if you revenge, you might bring more harm than expected and later regret at the end.

One man by the name of Emmanuel N Tshuma once went through a situation whereby one of his classmates slapped him on his cheek during his primary school years. Instead of him turning the other cheek to his classmate he decided to take revenge. Since it was a male and female involved, Emmanuel decided to fight back, those days Emmanuel was short whilst the girl was more stronger and taller than him, when Emmanuel prepared to launch his first fist on the girl, she grabbed Emmanuel by the collar of his school shirt and threw him few meters ahead, she kicked Emmanuel and many students who were watching laughed very hard, if at all Emmanuel didn't revenge he would not have been beaten like that. Revenge must be avoided so that we do not give the enemy a chance to interfere and use that as a weapon that will he will use to destroy us spiritually. Revenge should be avoided by self-control and laying our trust on God to fight for us because He never fails.

L. Love of Money

Money has started being a means of trade from the past till now in this present world. The truth is there is nothing wrong with using money because we need it in order to survive, without money there is no life. The danger part of money comes when we start having excessive love of it, when we do so, negative thoughts, ideas and plans begin to arise which will at the end of the day destroy our positive thinking. The enemy uses the love of money as a weapon to destroy Christians because he knows that everyone needs money, it is easier to convince someone to do something as long as money will be given to them in return as appreciation. People have a tendency of doing wrong things in favour of money which is not good; it completely damages our relationship with God. Let us have a look on a couple of verses in the Bible that talk about money.

Ps 37:16 a little that a righteous man hath is better than the riches of many wicked.

Proverbs 15:16 better is little with the fear of the LORD than great treasure and trouble therewith.

Ecclesiastes 5:10 He that loveth silver shall not be satisfied with silver; nor he that loveth abundance with increase: this is also vanity.

1Ti 6:10 for the love of money is the root of all evil: which while some coveted after, they have erred from the faith, and pierced

The bible condemns the love of money because indeed it is the root of all evil, it is time for us to understand that the love of money is never good and will never be good, we have to avoid loving money so that the enemy will not be able to setting a trap against us and defeat us with this powerful weapon. Below are some of the situations classified by Dawn Wilson which will identify you as a lover of money, if they are its time for you to learn a lesson and shift your ways.

- You become obsessed with becoming rich

- You never have enough

- You are living beyond your means

- You are becoming a show off

- You are characterized by greed.

- You have forgotten the source

- Your loyalties are divided.

- You are tempted to sin.

- Your life is starting to suffer

- You are wondering if you need counsel. (Wilson, 2016) (Morris, 25 April 2012)

These are the 10 signs that show that you love money too much, if any of the points match what you are going through it is time to pick yourself and escape from the love of money because it can destroy your life and even block your blessings from coming, The

Lord is calling all those who are heavy , He is calling all those who are burdened so that He can give them a better life, it is a matter of surrendering yourself unto The Lord asking Him to give you strength for He never fails.

M. Abuse

Abuse is referred to as treating someone or something the way that is not good causing pain and harm. Abuse is always hurtful and it will always be like that until the world comes to an end, there are many cases of abuse in this world, there is a lot of pain being caused through abuse, people hurt each other, people fight each other as well as killing each other through abuse, if not dealt with accordingly abuse can cause so much harm and danger not only to ourselves but the community at large. Abuse is one of the weapons used by the enemy to cause destruction. There are many different kinds of abuse but the top two recognized ones are physical abuse, emotional abuse and sexual abuse.

Physical abuse: It is referred to abuse that is involved in beating an individual to an extent that is over the limit, there are instances whereby couples abuse each other, wives beating their husbands or husbands beating their wives, parents beating their children to a point that is over the limit (Note: there is nothing wrong in beating a child when he/she has done something wrong but when the beating is done in a harsh manner that will not bring good results). Physical abuse is also found at school, at work, in the neighbourhood and elsewhere, the truth is that physical abuse is wrong and should be stopped.

Emotional abuse: This is a situation whereby words are uttered harshly to an individual causing pain in the heart. Emotional abuse takes place at home whereby parents speak harshly to their kids, husbands uttering harsh words to their wives, wives uttering harsh words to their husbands;

we see emotional abuse also being found at school, whereby teachers speak harshly to students, causing pain and embarrassment to children and that should be stopped.

Sexual abuse: This is a situation whereby an individual is mistreated in a sexual way, there are instances whereby an individual has no power to defend himself or herself which makes someone superior than them take advantage and use them sexually knowing that they will not be caught, this is an act of evil and it should be demolished, people doing such acts are going to get bad consequences one day, sexual abuse should be stopped.

The Bible strictly condemns abuse. The book of Exodus 21:20 encourages us on these words 'And if a man smite his servant, or his maid, with a rod, and he die under his hand; he shall be surely punished'. The Lord is going to punish all who abuse others, it is very painful to be abused, people who go through abuse live painful and miserable lives, and we must help each other in the world and be mature enough to live in peace without abusing and hurting each other's feelings. It is time to disappoint the enemy by saying no to abuse, people must also work together in fighting this weapon and defeating it, issues of abuse that are found should be dealt with well in time before they lead to further dangerous situations including killings, injuries and violence.

N. Stealing

Stealing is the act of taking something that does not belong to one without asking for permission. Stealing is very dangerous; it is categorized as one of the things that are dangerously done in secret. Stealing leads to theft and loss of trust. If not controlled at an early stage it might lead to dangerous crimes such as robbery and other related crimes in the future. It is the responsibility of parents, teachers and even us to teach children at a young age to avoid stealing before it is too late so that we create a free future generation. Thieves in this present world did not make themselves become like that on purpose but they lacked someone who could show them the dangers of stealing whilst they were young. Stealing is a bad habit that can even lead to prison. Emmanuel N Tshuma categorizes stealing in 4 levels.

Low class stealing: This is stealing that involved mainly at home, it is whereby one of the family members steals small things like sugar, food, or any small items that are not of great concern without the knowledge of others. This kind of stealing might lead to level two if not taken seriously.

Level two middle class stealing: Mainly takes place at home, school and at the workplace, it is when an individual steals things like money in wallets, or even things that have been forgotten by the owner without his knowledge, those kind of things are not identified until they are realised to be missing or when someone breaks the secret.

Level three medium class stealing: Takes place when big things are stolen in the community, at home, school and at the workplace, this is when things such as money expensive things like phones, laptops and even valuable items are stolen, this kind of stealing normally qualifies to be reported at the police station and it becomes a case.

High class maximum stealing: This is when now the lifestyle of the individual is theft, the individual gets to a point of even using weapons to threaten to kill or even killing just because of money, this is a very dangerous stage because stealing becomes a career and it makes the individual be more vulnerable to prison and even injury or being killed when caught.

The bible condemns stealing, it is also found in the one of the Ten Commandments. The book of Exodus 20:15 teaches us 'You shall not steal'. Stealing has never been good and it will never be good. We have to learn to avoid taking things without asking for permission or else they will make us do more theft in the coming time. Stealing makes people lose trust on an individual, and the sad part of trust is that when it is broken, it will not be mended again. Therefore it is wise to educate and teach each other on the dangers of stealing. It is high time people stand up and working together in establishing a future generation that will not be stealing. A future generation that will be walking freely in the streets never worrying about a thief that will come and steal from them. A future generation whereby escorts and security guards will not be needed because everyone will be honest and trusted, together we can make it in building a future like that through the help of our Lord Jesus Christ.

O. Unplanned Events

Unplanned events are referred to as events that come unplanned. They normally bring stress and pain. They always lead to people running around looking for assistance financially, emotionally, materially and spiritually. They come as a surprise and they demand attention. Unplanned events are dangerous because they make an individual lose hope and trust. They bring permanent memories that last the whole of a lifetime and can also get to a point of leading to trauma if not dealt with in time. The enemy gets excited in such events because that is where he gets a chance to challenge people especially Christians that God is there for them. Below are some of the examples of the common unplanned events in the world.

Funerals: When death occurs, it happens unplanned and this means that many tasks are to be taken, family members or the bereaved are forced to look start planning for the funeral as well as seeking for support, this brings strain on them and during this difficult time it is hard to trust that God really exists. The book of Ecclesiastes chapter 3 states that life will always change, there will always be a time to be born and a time to die, a time to laugh and a time to cry, a time to sow and a time to reap.

Accidents: Accidents at home, at the workplace, road, railway, sea and air accidents have become a great concern in the whole world, they have caused permanent injuries, high financial costs and even death. This has left many hopeless, only one can save us from all these and He is God the Creator of the heaven and the earth, our greatest cry to God every day is to ask Him to guide us wherever we go and protect us and our families at all times because we are living in a dangerous world.

Break-ups: We live in a world whereby many things are happening, friendships falling apart, relationships falling apart, couples divorcing each other, passion killings taking place, all these happen because of lack of trust and faithfulness, victims of breakups are never happy, some of them even go to a point of committing suicide, some fall into depression and stress, things become so tough and this on its own drags a person away from God , going to church becomes history to some of the victims of break ups because they feel that it is the end of life for them.

Unplanned events are of great concern in the modern society; the truth will remain the fact that there is nothing we can do to stop unplanned events from taking place. The only thing that we can do at this present moment is to trust in God always. The Lord says we should worry not for what tomorrow will bring but we should lay our trust on our Creator. It is very important to wake up every day in the morning just to ask The Lord to protect and guide us before the day starts, that on its own is very powerful and it can save us from many unplanned things that can happen throughout the day. Let us not allow the enemy to use unplanned events as a weapon to distract us from The Lord.

Spiritual Weapons Used By The Enemy To Defeat Christians In This World

The Ten Deadly Sins Commited By The Mouth

One pastor by the name of Robert Morris taught a very powerful topic entitled 'The ten deadly sins that are committed by the mouth', they are called deadly because they might seem to look small but deep down causing danger to our spiritual lives, let us have a look at the ten deadly sins:

1. Lying

Lying is defined as saying something that is not true. Lying is one of the easiest sins that are done in this present world. It is very easy to lie to someone yet knowing what the truth is. One important thing we should is that we tell a lie, we move from the throne of truth and we move to the throne of lies. A simple lie can damage a lot of things the same way a single matchstick can destroy thousands of trees. We must be careful with the words that we say to others either good or bad because it is absolutely impossible to forget or cancel what you just said. Emmanuel N Tshuma classifies lying in 7 different levels.

A) **Level 1:** You lie. It is a simple lie that is spoken at any minute at any time.

B) **Level 2:** This is whereby lying is done often when telling simple lies.

C) **Level 3**: It is whereby lying is done in serious issues that need questioning.

D) **Level 4**: This is whereby most people recognize you as a liar and never tolerate listening to you even if you present to them a valid situation.

E) **Level 5**: This is lying tempting at leadership level, it is whereby you tell a lie to a large group of people who are going to listen and be convinced.

F) **Level 6**: It is whereby lying becomes a lifestyle, to a point that you can even sugar-coat the lie by saying a little truth that is convincing.

G) **Level 7:** This is a serious level of lying where you can even do some serious deals that threaten the society; it is called obtaining by false pretences by the police.

We must avoid lying at all costs and try to say what is right. The Bible itself condemns lying. The book of Proverbs 12:19 says 'Truthful lips endure for ever, but a lying tongue is but for a moment'. The book of Proverbs 19:5 says 'A false witness will not go unpunished, and he who utters lies will not escape'. Lying has many bad and painful consequences, we must learn to say the truth at all times so that we do not fall in the pit of lies, because if we fall on it, chances of coming out are very low, May The good Lord deliver us from lying and give us the strength to say the truth always wherever we go and whatever we do in life.

2. Gossip

Gossip is referred to as talking about someone else in their absence to someone or a group of people. Gossip takes place everywhere in the world, it is found at the workplace, at home, at school, at church and the community at large. The truth about gossip is that he who gossips with you will gossip about you even in your absence. We must never tolerate gossip and say NO to it.

Gossip is dangerous to our spiritual lives, it is a weapon used by the enemy to destroy relationships between Christians. If not controlled it can even divide groups of people in church or even the church at large. There are instances whereby church members gossip about their leaders, in doing so this creates space for hate on their leaders and that comes to a point of affecting others as well and at the end it ends up causing hate and other unpleasant things.

The church must be the safest place for members to tell their secrets to, but when members are not loyal to each other and they begin spreading news of another person to others, it becomes a problem, that person who is being gossiped can end up being hurt and end up leaving church or even stopping to be a believer of Christ, such things should be known and controlled before it is too late. Members should develop trust on one another in order to build a faithful and loyal church. Let us have a look on a couple of verses that talk about gossip below:

Proverbs 14:23 in all toil there is profit, but mere talk tends only to want.

Proverbs 16:28 A perverse man spreads strife, and a whisperer separates close friends.

Jeremiah 9:4 Let everyone beware of his neighbour, and put no trust in any brother; for every brother is a supplanter, and every neighbour goes about as a slanderer.

Micah 7:5 Put no trust in a neighbour, have no confidence in a friend; guard the doors of your mouth from her who lies in your bosom.

The bible does not support gossip at all. The Word of God encourages us to be careful to who we tell our secrets to ,because even your closest relative, friend or worker can gossip about you or even use that to control you and threaten to tell others if you disappoint him/her, we must be careful of such people in this life. Gossip was never good in the past, it is not good in our present life and it will not be good in the future. Our aim should be to create a nation that does not gossip at all because gossip brings more problems than we can ever imagine, families have broken down through gossip, churches have been divided through gossip, relationships and friendships have failed because of gossip, jobs have been lost through gossip, buildings and furniture's have been destroyed because of gossip. Let us avoid gossip at all costs.

3. Slander

Slander is a situation in which someone or people spread rumours about someone that are not true. Some people define slander as a false spoken statement determined to damage the good opinion people have about someone or something. Slander is taking place in various areas throughout the world. People talk false statements about one another damaging the reputation of them. Slander is also found on the internet, people talk various story concerning people and some things, this makes some people believe the stories and others end up disagreeing with such stories. Slander is not good because it damages people's repetitions, a good example is in the church, the pastor might call a meeting with the board and tell them about someone who could be an assistant to the pastor after the meeting, if at all one member who is not the board's favourite is selected, they might meet together and try by all means to convince the pastor to never select him as his assistant by uttering stories that are untrue about him, we call that slandering. People who slander are going to be punished by God. Let us have a look on a couple of verses in the Bible that talk about Slander:

Psalms 31:13 Yea, I hear the whispering of many--terror on every side! --as they scheme together against me, as they plot to take my life.

Psalms 50:20 you sit and speak against your brother; you slander your own mother's son.

Proverbs 10:18 He who conceals hatred has lying lips, and he who utters slander is a fool.

I Timothy 3:11 the women likewise must be serious, no slanderers, but temperate, faithful in all things.

The Bible does not agree with slander, people who slander others are not worthy to be called friends, they cannot be trusted and we must be careful of such people in life. It is very painful to see marriages, friendships and relationships being broken because of slander, it is so hurtful and painful to come across couples and a friend fighting each other because of slander, God is going to punish slanderers very severely because of their evil act. Slander is a very evil act that is also associated with jealousy.

People must learn to avoid spreading rumours about other people before knowing the truth. It is better to keep quiet than talk about something that you are unsure about. That is the mistake that people make, it is funny to see how many people slander through the internet, what people must know about the internet is that not everything is true there. We must be careful on the way we research on the internet and we must be mature enough to understand what is true and what is not true, that will save us. Slander is one of the weapons used by the enemy on Christians, the enemy knows that if he uses this weapon in church, groups are going to develop and the church will not grow, it is time to avoid slander at all costs and teach about it at church.

4. Tale-Bearing

Tale bearing is a situation in which an individual or a group of people goes around spreading stories about people or other things that may be true or untrue. Tale-bearing breaks confidence and causes the victim who is being talked about to feel insecure. One good example is a situation in which one of the members in church has a successful company, then it happens that the owner wins a tender, he /she may decide to buy some good looking cars, whilst this is happening, one of the church members who is not happy about the success of the business may decide to go around spreading lies to other church members claiming who that owner think he or she is going around being prideful. We should be careful of such people in church because their mission is to destroy other people's repetition. Let us take a look on what a couple of verses in the Bible say about tale bearing.

Proverbs 17:9 He who forgives an offense seeks love, but he who repeats a matter alienates a friend.

Ezekiel 22:9 there are men in you who slander to shed blood, and men in you who eat upon the mountains; men commit lewdness in your midst.

Luke 24:11 but these words seemed to them an idle tale, and they did not believe them.

Proverbs 11:13 He who goes about as a talebearer reveals secrets, but he who is trustworthy in spirit keeps a thing hidden.

The Bible strictly condemns tale-bearing. People who reveal secrets about people that are not supposed to be known are untrusted and cannot be relied on. Tale bearing should be taught in churches, schools and businesses because it does not bring any value to the community as large. It does not contribute to spiritual growth as well. It is difficult to worship and sing praises freely in church when you realise that people talk about you, such acts should not be allowed in church. Places such as the church should be places of safety and trust that people should present their problems and weaknesses without being judged. If we judge people and reveal their secrets in church, next time they, might prefer telling their secrets to other people who might be a bad influence.

It is high time that things start being done the right way. The best medicine to cure tale-bearing is to avoid people who talk the secrets of others in their absence. The best remedy is to refuse to listen to such stories and tell the people that you are not interested, if we begin to entertain them they might as well go around and tell others that they were with you when they told the secrets about other people which will in turn damage your own repetition so it is better to run away and step back from such cases. We must embarrass the enemy by destroying this weapon called tale-bearing, in that way we will establish a society and churches that are the best in handling people's matters without any fear of disappointments.

5. Sowing Discord

Sowing discord refers to disagreeing on someone or something as well as quarrelling. In this modern world we come across different people who always quarrel and never agree with what others say. People who sow discord are always talkative people. They spend the time talking too much to a point whereby they can convince people to listen to them and follow them. They have strong skills that they use to win people in their arguments. Some of the dangerous people that sow discord can win a debate when they are alone against as many as ten people. Such people are very dangerous because the strong way they convince can lead to many people astray. There are some people who always disagree with the decisions and ideas that are being suggested by others, they are always negative and are always the first to criticise if at all the idea or decision carried out in the meeting did not succeed. Church leaders must be careful enough to locate such people in the church early in time before they cause serious harm to the church. Let us take a look on different verses that talk about sowing discord.

Psalms 35:20 For they do not speak peace, but against those who are quiet in the land they conceive words of deceit.

Proverbs 6:14-15 with perverted heart devises evil, continually sowing discord; therefore calamity will come upon him suddenly; in a moment he will be broken beyond healing.

Proverbs 29:9 If a wise man has an argument with a fool, the fool only rages and laughs, and there is no quiet.

Proverbs 21:19 it is better to live in a desert land than with a contentious and fretful woman.

In the hospital, nurses and doctors will not tolerate an employee who sows discord to other workers, in business the manager will not be pleased to see his/her employee sowing discord with other employees in the company. The same way this is happening God will not allow people who sow discord to continue doing that in the church. The church is the wife of Christ therefore it has to be respected, God will punish those who always quarrel and mock others. The book of Proverbs 6:15 covers this point of calamity. This refers to an event that causes harm or damage. The Bible confirms that people who sow discord will be severely punished. The enemy uses the weapon of sowing discord to confuse the people in church so that they do not understand each other when discussing important things. Therefore it is our duty as Christians to work together in building strong churches in which people are united.

The world will be an awesome place to live in if at all we did not have people who sow discord, but it is possible to create a place like that. It is going to need me and you to make a difference through the help of our Creator of the heaven and the earth.

6. Cursing

Pastor Robert Morris defines cursing as a word or phrase that has a magic power to make something bad happen or a rude or offensive word that people use when they are very angry. Cursing is not good at all because it can tear your life down. People who curse others are never happy, people who are cursed are not happy at all because they live miserable lives. No matter how bad you can ever get in life, you should not even once curse yourself because that can happen the same way you said, words that you speak have power and they can either build you up or tear you down.

In this present life we see Christians getting out of control when they are hurt or angry, they start cursing their businesses, they curse their families, they curse their friends, they curse their debit cards and they curse their own lives. People should never utter this word ' I will never make it in life' This paraphrase on its own can set a permanent scar that will tear your life down until you start talking good news about your life. When you are living in destruction and you start proclaiming good things by faith, great and mighty things are going to happen in your life through the blood of Jesus Christ. Let us take a look at a couple of verses that talk about Cursing:

Job 2:9-10 then his wife said to him, "Do you still hold fast your integrity? Curse God, and die. "But he said to her, "You speak as one of the foolish women would speak. Shall we receive good at the hand of God, and shall we not receive evil?" In all this Job did not sin with his lips.

Ps 109:17 He loved to curse; let curses come on him! He did not like blessing; may it be far from him!

Mal 3:9 you are cursed with a curse, for you are robbing me; the whole nation of you.

Mt 5:44 But I say to you, Love your enemies and pray for those who persecute you.

Jas 3:10 From the same mouth come blessing and cursing. My brethren, this ought not to be so.

The Bible explains itself clearly that all those who curse, let them be cursed and all those who speak blessings are going to be blessed. The Bible encourages us to be like Job, tis man lost everything; he lost everything to appoint that his family, friends and the community questioned about his Saviour, he never ever uttered a curse upon his life but at the end he reaped good blessings in his life. If we start speaking positive things in our lives, they will start happening, we must avoid giving up too soon and letting the enemy play around with cursing in our hearts, but let us establish a daily lifestyle of speaking good things to each other. Cursing should be stopped by everyone before we fall victims of the enemy.

7. Blasphemy

Blasphemy refers to a language that insults or shows lack of respect to God. There are people in this world that insult God and some come to a point of showing lack of respect to God as well. Blasphemy is a serious sin that is punishable to God. As people we must learn to control ourselves when we are very hurt or very angry or either very happy when we involve God in our situations. In other words the name of The Lord should not be used in vain. We are living in a world whereby there are fake pastors, prophets , evangelists, apostles or teachers, we should be careful of such people, they go around in sheep's clothing pretending to be used by God but deep down being wolves doing the works of the enemy, they are considered as very dangerous. Some pretend to convince a person that God told them this and that which makes people to be forced to accept because it is difficult to refuse to listen to someone who claims they have been sent by God. Let us take a look on what the Bible says about blasphemy:

Leviticus 24:16 He who blasphemes the name of the LORD shall be put to death; all the congregation shall stone him; the sojourner as well as the native, when he blasphemes the Name, shall be put to death.

Isaiah 52:5 now therefore what have I here, says the LORD, seeing that my people are taken away for nothing? Their rulers wail, says the LORD, and continually all the day my name is despised.

Mark 3:29 but whoever blasphemes against the Holy Spirit never has forgiveness, but is guilty of an eternal sin".

Exodus 20:7 "You shall not take the name of the LORD your God in vain; for the LORD will not hold him guiltless who takes his name in vain."

People who do not respect God or insult Him will be punished.

We must avoid blasphemy at all costs and even warn those who insult or use the name of The Lord in vain.

8. Filthy Language

This refers to language that is not acceptable at all which covers anger, blasphemy, malice, wrath and other things. Let us look closely in what the Bible says:

James 1:8 a double minded man is unstable in all his ways.

Colossians 3:8 But now ye also put off all these; anger, wrath, malice, blasphemy, filthy communication out of your mouth.

We are going to explain the book of Colossians 3:8 by explaining what each word means.

Anger: Being furious about something to a point that it takes away happiness leading to being pained and hurt.

Wrath: This is referred to as extreme anger; it leads to destruction and might also lead to injury if at all fighting is involved.

Malice: A feeling of hatred for somebody that causes a desire to harm them.

Blasphemy: Disrespect towards God.

Filthy communication: Corrupt language that can tear down spiritually.

We are warned in the book of Colossians 3:8 to stay away from anger, wrath, malice, blasphemy and filthy language. These things can tear us down spiritually and put us away from God thus we should be careful when we are affected by them. The enemy uses these weapons to destroy Christians; this is so serious because even Christians in leadership level like pastors and church leaders can ruin their spiritual life through filthy language. It is never easy to escape from filthy language because there will always be people who will challenge you in your personal life. There are situations in which church members get angry to a point that they leave church, others are affected by unplanned events such as breakups and funerals then they decide to backslide from church because they feel so much hurt and neglected by God, others get to a point of damaging properties before leaving for good knowing that they will not come back again to the place they were hurt.

Filthy language should be taught often in churches because many Christians are lost through this weapon, this weapon has secretly destroyed powerful Christians who would have made a huge difference if at all they did not leave church, but unfortunately through the power of the enemy they went out from serving God. Christians should control the way they get angry not in church alone but at home, at school and in the community at large, as Christians we are here to inspire others to come to Christ, what will be the point of being Christians worshiping God but yet we are poor in controlling our temper? We are here in the world to make a difference, to show others that it is possible to live a life without anger, wrath, malice, blasphemy and filthy language.

9. Contentious Speech

This refers to Hurtful, hateful, malicious, disagreeable, argumentative behaviour. Let us have a look at several scriptures in the Bible that talk about contentious speech:

Proverbs 26:21 as coals are to burning coals, and wood to fire; so is a contentious man to kindle strife.

Proverbs 15:18 A wrathful man stireth up strife; but he that is slow to anger appeaseth strife.

There are people who love to argue always, some are always hurtful and disagree all the time; such people are not to be trusted. People who are contentious are very dangerous, just as mentioned in this booklet, we are fighting a spiritual world war and we do not need contentious people who will distract us whilst we are fighting with the enemy and his team. Below are some of the dangers of contentious speech.

- Contentious speech makes the victim hurt, these people have a habit of uttering words that bring pain to the individual or the group of people; they think they are smart enough to say whatever they want to say at their own time because of their talking skills.

- Contentious speech makes people hate each other, when people do not love each other; the enemy hops in to create further havoc and problems which might break the unity and bond that was there in the first place. Hate is very dangerous as it can bring many other bad things like jealousy and wrath.

- Contentious speech brings strife. This is referred to as an angry or violent disagreement between two people or groups of people. This is one of the areas that are very dangerous involving contentious speech; this is very dangerous because it can cause two or more large groups to fight each other which might contribute to further injuries as a result.

People who have a habit of calling large groups of people then they begin uttering words that do not bring peace but violence should be rebuked because they threaten the inner peace of the community as well as the church. Places like churches should also be extra careful of those kinds of people, they are so harmful such that they can divide the church of God and even try to collapse it. One of the most important prayer points that should be taken into consideration in our homes and the church at large is to ask God to help us establish church and families that are free from contentious speech in order to create an environment that will have peace as well as a platform that will have people having one mind and mission. A powerful church is made up of strong leaders that agree with each other instead of criticizing, mocking and hating each other.

10. Unbelief

Unbelief is a state of not believing, some define it as inability to believe. Unbelief is a weapon that we must be aware of, it blinds the minds of people so that they don't get a chance to experience the power beyond belief. Let us look on a couple of verses below that talk about unbelief and how they affected various people in The Bible.

- Exodus 5:2 But Pharaoh said, "Who is the LORD, that I should heed his voice and let Israel go? I do not know the LORD, and moreover I will not let Israel go." Pharaoh did not want to believe in God, he had unbelief and held the Israelites in captivity until God punished him severely by demolishing most of his army at the Red Sea.

- Matthew 13:58 and he did not do many mighty works there, because of their unbelief. Whilst Jesus Christ was travelling in different areas preaching and performing miracles, He came across a certain place where people had unbelief, He left them and did not do any miracles there, and those people missed blessings from Jesus.

- 2Co 6:14 Do not be mismated with unbelievers. For what partnership have righteousness and iniquity? Or what fellowship has light with darkness? The apostle Paul warns us to be careful when we are with unbelievers, their mission is to put believers into darkness by tempting them to do what is opposed by the light; we must be mature enough to have a stand when we are in the midst of situations like that and trust in The Lord always.

- Hebrews 3:12 Take care, brethren, lest there be in any of you an evil, unbelieving heart, leading you to fall away from the living God. Unbelievers are considered as evil because a person who does not believe in God is associated as the opposition team which is supported by the enemy himself the devil, it is our duty as Christians to encourage others to live a new life with God, because He is real and He is the omnipotent, omniscience and eternal.

- Numbers 13:2 "Send men to spy out the land of Canaan, which I give to the people of Israel; from each tribe of their fathers shall you send a man, everyone a leader among them." 12 spy's were sent in the promised land and when they came back , 10 spy's gave a negative report , the Bible calls that unbelief only two of them gave a positive report that is faith.

Dangers of Unbelief

At certain times people are unaware of the dangers that unbelief can bring, people tend to speak words that are rough and some even get to a point of even disrespecting God, since the enemy has blinded the minds of many people in the world, some people end up crossing into the red line which is provoking God just because they don't believe in God, people should be careful with the words they utter: Let us take a look on what the book of Galatians 6:7 says.

Ga 6:7 Be not deceived; God is not mocked: for whatsoever a man soweth, that shall he also reap.

Below are some of the people who mocked God, but because of what they sowed they ended up reaping disaster and pain. This information was written by Johnny Black Hayden. (Hayden, 2016)

- John Lennon (1940-1980) said that Christianity will go in 1966, he continued to say that it would vanish and shrink, and that he was more popular than Jesus. Fourteen years later Lennon was shot dead.

- Tancredo Neves (President of Brazil) during the presidential campaign he said that if he got 500 000 votes from his party, not even God would remove him from the presidency. He ended up getting the votes but he got sick the day before becoming a president and he died.

- Cazuza (Bi-sexual Brazilian composer, singer and poet): During a show in Canecio (Rio de Janeiro) while smoking cigarette, studies indicate that he puffed some smoke into the air and said 'God, that's for you'. He died at the age of 32 of lung cancer in a horrible manner.

- The man who built the titanic: After the construction of the Titanic, a reporter asked him how safe the Titanic would be, with an ironic tone he said 'Not even God would sink it'; we all know what happened to the Titanic.

- Marilyn Monroe (Actress) she was visited by Billy Graham during a presentation of a show. He said the spirit of God had sent him to preach to her. After hearing what the preacher said, she replied 'I don't need your Jesus'. A week later she was found dead in her apartment.

We should be careful with the words we say when we are around people because if we cannot control ourselves we might end up cursing our lives just simply because we uttered a word that disrespected God. We must never allow the enemy to use the weapon of unbelief on us no matter how hard and challenging life may be and no matter how hurt you are in life.

Deadly Sins Commited In Various Areas Of Our Spiritual Lives

1. Anger

Anger refers to a situation in which someone is hurt because of a feeling of disappointment that has been done to them. Everyone has been angry, being angry takes away happiness and makes our mood down, it enables the heart to beat faster and it makes a person feel uncomfortable, people have various ways in which they get angry, some of them decide to keep quiet, some shout at other people, some decide to destroy things, some decide to fight. Everyone gets angry and one thing that we have to learn is that we should be careful with the way we get angry, because anger is just one letter away from danger.

There are many bad situations that have happened through anger, lack of controlled anger creates a room for further damage thus we have to learn to control it always. It is okay to be angry but we have to learn to control our anger, if we do not learn to control our anger we may end up doing things that we will later regret in the future. Lack of control of anger can lead to the following:

Relationship break-up: In a relationship if the girlfriend and boyfriend always argue when they are angry , the relationship will never last, they should solve matters peacefully and try to control the way they act when they are angry.

Divorce: If anger lasts for a long period in a family, it may lead to divorce, no man and woman can afford spending his/her entire lifetime in fear of his/her partner making their life miserable through anger.

Damage to infrastructure: Lack of controlled anger leads to damage of things, most often people damage things they later regret about. People have a tendency of breaking their phones, damaging property, cars just to mention a few. Property is expensive.

Loss of job: Lack of controlled anger may lead to loss of job; no employer can afford an employee who is always angry at work. People who are always angry slowdown business and they may make business slow down. People must learn to control their temper always not only at work but at church, at home and in the community at large.

Injury: People who get very angry may end up getting involved in a fight. The exchanging of fists and slapping can lead to more serious anger called wrath which is even more harmful than ever. People must avoid getting into fights when they are angry.

The Bible condemns lack of control of anger. The Word of God tells us to be angry but we should not sin. The Book of Matthew 5:22 says 'But I say to you that everyone who is angry with his brother shall be liable to judgment; whoever insults his brother shall be liable to the council, and whoever says, 'You fool!' shall be liable to the hell of fire'. The book of Ephesians 4:26 says 'Be angry but do not sin; do not let the sun go down on your anger'. Let us never allow the enemy to hinder us with this weapon of anger.

2. Laziness

Laziness is a situation in which someone does not do a specific thing without any valid reason. Laziness is a weapon that is used by the enemy to slow down progress. There are many people who would have been doctors, engineers, pastors, bishops, millionaires or even billionaires if they were serious about their goals, but due to the fact that they did not motivate themselves enough, they would have achieved their missions. We must be extra careful of this weapon. This weapons operates in a secret way but the danger part is in the future when you will begin the remember dozens of opportunities that you had whilst you had the opportunity. It is better to waste no time and start turning our laziness into something better. Let us take a look on some scriptures in the Bible that talk about Laziness:

Proverbs 10:4 a slack hand causes poverty, but the hand of the diligent makes rich.

Proverbs 28:19 He who tills his land will have plenty of bread, but he who follows worthless pursuits will have plenty of poverty.

Ephesians 4:28 Let the thief no longer steal, but rather let him labor, doing honest work with his hands, so that he may be able to give to those in need.

1 Timothy 5:13 besides that, they learn to be idlers, gadding about from house to house, and not only idlers but gossips and busybodies, saying what they should not.

The Bible strictly condemns laziness; God does not want a person to sit down and expect to be spoon fed without doing something. At least we should try rather than sitting doing nothing at all. A lazy person cannot be selected as a church leader, a president or a business manager because it looks obvious that things are going to suffer. We should not allow ourselves to be supervised all the time but we should learn to work under no supervision so that we show others how mature we are. Being a hard worker has many benefits. People who are hardworking are very successful in life, most of them get married and are married, some are millionaires some are successful businessman and businesswoman. If at all you are lazy it is time to get back up, motivate yourself and start planning about your life. If at all you are not working or sit all day at home, it is time for you to write down your goals start thinking of what you can do in life, some people are in hospitals, some are wishing to get an opportunity like the one you have now, get up and do something before time runs out. One day we will not have that opportunity so we have to use the little time that we have to make a difference.

We are victorious through Christ Jesus. The Lord will always be there for those who try their best to succeed, people who are not lazy but people who would rather strain themselves to do the best that they can to make a difference in their lives.

3. Discontentment

Discontentment refers to a situation whereby someone is unsatisfied with what they have. Many people are unsatisfied in their lives, they spend time unhappy thinking of how other people are better than them and this pains them severely. This life that we are living is too short for unhappiness thus we should be content with what we have. Discontentment seems to be a universal problem. Below are the sayings of some famous people who lived on earth many years ago according to Woodrow Kroll:

Socrates (469-399 BC) the famous Greek philosopher who is credited with the development of western philosophy, said "Contentment is natural wealth, luxury is artificial poverty."

Epicurus lived 341-270 BC. He was an ancient Greek philosopher and the founder of the school of philosophy called Epicureanism. Epicurus said, "If thou wilt make a man happy, add not unto his riches but take away from his desires."

Seneca was a Roman Stoic philosopher and statesman. He lived 4 BC to AD 64. He was tutor and later advisor to Emperor Nero. Seneca said, "It is not the man who has too little, but the man who craves more, that is poor."

There are two types of discontentment, and these are good and bad. The good discontentment is situations in which you are unsatisfied with the way you are lazy to do some things or not being able to achieve some things. There is also bad discontentment in which you spend time worrying about other people's success. (Note that there is a difference between jealousy and discontentment. Jealousy is when you hate other people because of their success in life and chooses to be distant from them; discontentment is when you are only worried about the success of other people but not holding a grudge against them or hating them. Here is a couple of verses in the Bible that talk about Discontentment:

Philippians 4:11 not that I complain of want; for I have learned, in whatever state I am, to be content.

Psalms 37:7 Be still before the LORD, and wait patiently for him; fret not yourself over him who prospers in his way, over the man who carries out evil devices!

The Bible encourages us as people to be content with what we have, of course we will come through situations that will make us wish to live a good successful life like others but the truth of the situation is that our day will come, we just have to wait patiently on The Lord and never allow the enemy to use this weapon of discontentment to make our miserable taking away our inner joy.

4. Lust

Webster's 1828 defines lust as a longing desire; eagerness to possess or enjoy. It also defines lust as having a carnal desire; to desire eagerly the gratification of carnal appetite. Lust affects a person and it should be avoided. Lust removes a person from the physical nature to sexual nature causing the mind to start thinking of sexual cravings and strong sexual desires. Lust can be classified into two categories, which are lusting looking at physical appearance and looking on the internet and other electronic devices which is called pornography.

These two lusts have affected many people in a bad way because lust is very different from love. The danger part of lust is that a person can lust after another whilst having no feelings at all, that's one of the most dangerous things that have killed many relationships, lust only lasts for a certain period of time then with time it later fades and forces the mind to think of another appearance again which is more stronger than the one looked before. Below are some statistical findings by Woodrow Kroll (Kroll, 2012) concerning pornography.

Every second – $3,075 is being spent on pornography. Every second – 28,258 Internet users are viewing pornography. Every second – 372 Internet users are typing adult search terms into search engines. Every 39 minutes – a new pornographic video is being created in the United States. There are 4.2 million porn websites (12% of total websites).There are 420 million pornographic pages in existence today. There are 68 million daily pornographic search engine requests (that's 25%of total search engine requests).2.5 billion pornographic emails are sent and received every day.42.7% of Internet users view porn.

Lust is the engine that leads to several kinds of sexual immorality which are fornication, adultery, masturbation, same sex encounters, incest and many others, if only people would learn to control the way they lust or avoiding at all costs, there won't be any difficulties in this world that we are living in, but now since it's hard to control lust, it has led to many habits that are condemned by the Bible, let us have a look on what the Bible says about lust.

Deuteronomy 5:18 "Neither shall you commit adultery.

Matthew 5:28 But I say to you that everyone who looks at a woman lustfully has already committed adultery with her in his heart.

Galatians 5:17 For the desires of the flesh are against the Spirit, and the desires of the Spirit are against the flesh; for these are opposed to each other, to prevent you from doing what you would.

James 1:15 Then desire when it has conceived gives birth to sin; and sin when it is full-grown brings forth death.

The Word of God encourages us to flee from lust because it is sin. We are living in a world where we are exposed to different kinds of temptation, the young youth, wear whatever they like which leads to lust, people talk filthy language and contentious speech which lead to lust, everywhere people go there is always something that drives the mind to lust, it is time to wake up and know that lust can be avoided through walking not in the flesh but in the spirit.

5. Depression

Thinking too much to a point that ends up taking someone's peace of mind for a longer period of time leads to depression. This is a very dangerous state that can end up changing the lifestyle and behaviour permanently when not treated on time. People are depressed because of many things such as:

Failed relationships	Unpaid debts	Unplanned
pregnancy		
Failure at school or university		
Poverty	Abuse	
Death of a loved one	Divorce	Sickness and diseases
Rape	Political power	Expulsion from work
Business failure	Family disputes	Failure to use money wisely

The world is attacked because of many various reasons that end up leading to depression, Some end up being affected mentally, some end up committing suicide, some leave church, some leave their families, some live painful lives just because of depression, this is very dangerous and needs to be taken seriously, it is difficult to change the way of thinking of someone who is depressed as well trying to convince them that everything will be alright. Therefore it is vital for everyone in earth to help one another to ensure that depressed people are spotted well in time before it is too late.

The fact will remain the same, depressed people should learn only one thing, the fact that they are depressed will not change anything that happened before the state of depression took place in their lives, the only option is to accept the situation and move on. There is a saying that says 'Never give up', this phrase can save a life, there is no need of giving up in life whilst you are still breathing , the fact that you are living in earth today is a very great gift on its own, people never realise that, some people waste their time being depressed forgetting that some are in hospitals wishing to have an opportunity to be living healthy lives, forgetting that some are in injuries and they cannot even walk and try to change their lives, no matter is worth giving up on. Counsellors, pastors, social workers and the community are always available to help those who are depressed, if they feel that their situation is serious they should approach the above mentioned people as early as possible. Below are scriptures in the Bible that talk about depression.

Deuteronomy 1:21 Behold, the LORD your God has set the land before you; go up, take possession, as the LORD, the God of your fathers, has told you; do not fear or be dismayed.'

Isaiah 42:4 He will not fail or be discouraged till he has established justice in the earth; and the coastlands wait for his law.

The Bible strictly condemns depression, the Lord did not create people to come and be depressed on earth, He created people to come into the world and live with each other in peace remembering The King of Kings and worshipping Him in one accord happily, enjoying life abundantly and full of joy. Depression must be avoided.

6. Jealousy

Jealousy is the art of oneself being unhappy of the success of the other. This activity is found in the world and started as early as the time of Creation when Cain killed Abel because of his jealousy that his brother offered a better sacrifice to God than him. We are living in a world of jealousy. People envy one another, hate each other and others get to a point of killing each other just because of jealousy. The enemy uses jealousy to destroy Christians in church, the moment one looks at the success of another in church , he/she ends up being bored going to church this is very evil and it is associated with the acts of the devil. Emmanuel N Tshuma classifies jealousy in four main categories:

Inward jealousy: This is whereby people do not show you that they are jealous. They spend time smiling at you but deep down in their hearts having full of hate.

Outward Jealousy: It is whereby people physically show you that they are jealous, they avoid you at all costs and avoid being with you at all times.

Shallow jealousy: It is whereby people are jealous at you to a point that they hate you but they do not think of any negative ideas to plot against you.

Deep Jealousy: The most dangerous type in which people can plot to kill you because of your success, or even wish to injure you, or wish all kinds of evil plans to make sure that you do not succeed. This type of jealousy is almost aligned to witchcraft as it is only a step away.

The danger part of jealousy is that sometimes it is difficult to identify someone who is jealous on you, the best medicine for jealousy is to pray and ask God for His mercy every time, the other medicine of jealousy is to trust no one but yourself only. Your closest friend or relative or family member can be jealous at you therefore it is very vital to take care of your life all the time and ensure that you are safe at all, times. Here are some safety guidelines that will help protect us from jealousy:

- Galatians 5:26 encourages us saying ' Let us have no self-conceit, no provoking of one another, no envy of one another'.

- Be careful on the way you talk and do things at school, home, community, church and any other place, mind your tongue and learn what to say and not to say.

- Never show people your next move in life, never post your success on social media, WhatsApp, Instagram and many other social networks , they may be a gateway to jealousy, not everyone will be proud of your success.

- Always be careful when going with people and make sure you are alert on the way you cope with them anywhere, anytime.

- Couples and lovers should avoid posting their relationship status to other people either physically or on social networks. they should completely remove pride out because vultures will always be there to try and cause havoc

- Praying without ceasing cancels the spirit of jealousy sent to you, it is 100% reliable, no spirit is above God. Be more than careful in this present life.

7. Unforgiveness

Un-forgiveness is a situation whereby one is unable to forgive another on their past mistakes that are difficult to forget about. People have a lot of forgiveness problems especially when they were hurt beyond repair. One thing that people must understand about is that no matter how they refuse to forgive others that will never benefit them at all. The only option is to forgive. Let us browse through different scriptures that talk about forgiveness below:

Genesis 50:17 'Say to Joseph, Forgive, I pray you, the transgression of your brothers and their sin, because they did evil to you.' And now, we pray you, forgive the transgression of the servants of the God of your father." Joseph wept when they spoke to him.

Proverbs 20:22 Do not say, "I will repay evil"; wait for the LORD, and he will help you.

Matthew 5:24 leave your gift there before the altar and go; first be reconciled to your brother, and then come and offer your gift.

Matthew 18:21-22 Then Peter came up and said to him, "Lord, how often shall my brother sin against me, and I forgive him? As many as seven times?" Jesus said to him, "I do not say to you seven times, but seventy times seven.

Luke 6:35 But love your enemies, and do good, and lend, expecting nothing in return; and your reward will be great, and you will be sons of the Most High; for he is kind to the ungrateful and the selfish.

The Bible strictly condemns un-forgiveness, we are taught in the Bible to bless those who curse us, those who hurt us. We are taught on how Joseph forgave his brothers after they sold him out to slavery, we are taught on the dangers of un-forgiveness. We should learn to forgive others, one thing we must learn is that The Lord God forgives us each and every day when we commit sin, and it would therefore be unfair to refuse to forgive your brother or sister on earth. One of the dangers of un-forgiveness is that it can end up leading to one of the paths that take people to the lake of fire, a brother or sister in Christ who refuses to forgive another cannot be forgiven by God. Here is a story that warns us against un-forgiveness.

As Emmanuel N Tshuma came across several stories in the internet, he came across one story of a sister who was dead for few minutes but later came back to life, the story continues to say that whilst that sister was looking she was taken to heaven where she saw the most beautiful things that she ever saw in her life, then later on she was taken to hell where she saw continuous destruction, fire everywhere , people crying, the sad part is that as she began to study out she realised that others who were burning in hell where the most powerful Christians who lived on earth but lacked only one thing in their lives, and that is un-forgiveness, they were bitterly crying to be given a second chance to go back to earth and forgive those they refused to forgive. Moments later she came back to life and told many people this experience. People must be very careful in terms of forgiveness. God is watching and is waiting for you to forgive that person that you think you will not forgive anymore, the time is now, it is time to break that bond and forgive that person. Many people have blocked their blessings through un-forgiveness. It is time to fix that as early as possible.

8. Selfishness

Webster's Dictionary defines a selfish person as one "concerned excessively or exclusively with oneself." There are many people in this world that are selfish either at home, school, at the workplace or in the community at large. There are people who do not want to give others yet having more than enough. There is no use in living a good life owning everything yet your neighbour or friend is struggling and in need of something. Emmanuel N Tshuma classifies selfishness in two categories which are:

Inward selfishness: This is a kind of selfishness whereby one owns or has something but chooses to keep his/her things on secret. These kinds of people keep their things to themselves and never show or boast about them. Inward selfish people can walk on the street wearing like people who do not live wealthy lives but yet they are wealthy, they can get to a point of living a lifestyle that is right with the fear of showing themselves to others. They are normally of good character.

Outward selfishness: This is a kind of selfishness that involves people who are easily recognized to be having more than enough but yet they choose to be selfish and never bother helping others. They are difficult to deal with and it is very rare for them to associate with other people, they display a character that makes other people to be nervous in asking them for help.

Selfishness is never right, it makes an individual be far from the blessings of God, because The Lord has spoken in The Bible that He will bless the hand that giveth, we should learn to give so that God will give us more than what we gave. Let us take a look at a couple of verses in the Bible that talk about selfishness.

Proverbs 11:26 He that withholdeth corn, the people shall curse him: but blessing shall be upon the head of him that selleth it.

Hosea 10:1 Israel is an empty vine, he bringeth forth fruit unto himself: according to the multitude of his fruit he hath increased the altars; according to the goodness of his land they have made goodly

Matthew 25:43 I was a stranger, and ye took me not in: naked, and ye clothed me not: sick, and in prison, and ye visited me not.

Philippians 2:4 Look not every man on his own things, but every man also on the things of others.

The Bible condemns selfishness, it is a pity to realise and find out that many people in this present world only want to satisfy themselves without helping other people. People spend time enjoying themselves forgetting others, in church people want to show off the way they dress or give offerings without helping those in need, some on workplaces they choose to buy themselves food for lunch forgetting about those who cannot afford. There is always a reward for an individual that helps others whether you are a church goer or not whether you are wealthy or not wealthy. Selfishness is a weapon used by the enemy, it should be avoided.

9. Backsliding

Backsliding is a situation in which an individual decides to stop going to church or becoming poor spiritually but still going to church. The most dangerous form of backsliding is the one in which an individual stops going to church completely, this might be due to a couple of reasons like the ones mentioned below.

Unfair treatment by the church leader or any other member in the church	Refusal to be given several position(s) in church
Stealing in church and getting caught	Depression
Gossip	Family issues
Slander	Location to a place far from church
Tale bearing	Work issues
Change of lifestyle	Anger
Relationship break-ups/ friendship break-ups	Divorce

These are the several reasons why people backslide in church, Backsliding should be avoided at all costs because now it gives Satan an opportunity to play around with your life only to dump you when now your life will be torn into pieces and going to church being remembered as history. It is okay if at all work takes you far from your church but that doesn't mean that you can now change your lifestyle but in other words it says it's time to pray, read The Bible more and concentrate on God to the fullest, people have a tendency of forgetting that part. Let us take a look at some scriptures in The Bible that talk about backsliding.

Exodus 32:1 And when the people saw that Moses delayed to come down out of the mount, the people gathered themselves together unto Aaron, and said unto him, Up, make us gods, which shall go before us; for as for this Moses, the man that brought us up out of the land of Egypt, we wot not what is become of him.

Revelation 2:4 nevertheless I have somewhat against thee, because thou hast left thy first love.

2Peter 2:20 For if after they have escaped the pollutions of the world through the knowledge of the Lord and Saviour Jesus Christ, they are again entangled therein, and overcome, the latter end is worse with them than the beginning.

Luke 11:26 then goeth he, and taketh to him seven other spirits more wicked than himself; and they enter in, and dwell there: and the last state of that man is worse than the first.

Backsliding is a weapon used by the enemy to distract and destroy Christians, the enemy knows that if he involves gossip, anger, depression, hatred and several other bad things in church , some will decide to be more hurt and backslide, the enemy can also try to bring temptations knowing that the individual will end up falling in the trap and end up leaving church, we should be careful of these things because if we fail to control them they will control us and lead us into the lake of fire, rapture is coming, Jesus Christ is coming soon, He will only take the faithful and those who are tricked by the enemy will be left.

10. Worrying

Emmanuel N Tshuma defines worry as the process of imagining things that do not exist with the fear of what they will do in the future. People waste a lot of time being worried without realising that it actually takes away their happiness. When we worry we accomplish nothing at all,

people spend a lot of time during the day thinking about many things for example, thinking about paying bills, worrying about your distant family members and friends, worrying about what will happen tomorrow, worrying about your sickness, worrying about the way you are different from others, that is actually unusual. Most of the time you worry can be changed into something better, it is rather better to think of getting rich rather than thinking what you are going to eat tomorrow. The enemy uses worrying as a weapon to distract Christians in their spiritual lives and their walk with God. Christians who spend the time worrying find it very difficult to concentrate on church and even grow spiritually thus we must be careful on the way we worry too much.

We should not worry much because our Creator lives and He is there 24/7 whenever we need Him. Sometimes Christians worry to a point that God is ready to hear and listen to their problems anytime they need help. Let us look at a couple of verses in the Bible that talk about Worry:

Matthew 6:25 Therefore I say unto you, Take no thought for your life, what ye shall eat, or what ye shall drink; nor yet for your body, what shall ye put on. Is not the life more than meat, and the body than raiment?

Philippians 4:6 be careful for nothing; but in everything by prayer and supplication with thanksgiving let your requests be made known unto God.

2 Timothy 2:9 wherein I suffer trouble, as an evil doer, even unto bonds; but the word of God is not bound.

1 Peter 5:7 Casting all your care upon him; for he careth for you.

The Bible strictly tells us to avoid worrying too much because The Lord has told us to cast our troubles upon Him and He shall be there to support us always, people must understand that worrying is harmful in our lives spiritually, physically and mentally, it can take away a person's happiness and lead to depression and many other painful situations. 80% of the things we worry about never happen at all, that means worrying actually wastes time and eats most of the time we would have used to think about better things for our future. We must cast away our burdens unto The Lord so that He can sustain us, no problem is bigger than God because He is the Creator of the heavens and the earth, why should we waste our time worrying too much without asking Him to help us? Worry must be stopped in our lives.

Additional Weapons Used By The Enemy To Make Christians Lives Miserable

Some of the weapons used by the enemy are just meant to make Christian lives miserable, since the enemy does not enjoy watching peace and a joy in people's lives, his aim to involve certain things that will obviously remove the happiness of enjoying life and instead bring certain weapons that are going to cause confusion and certainly end up leading to a miserable life. We as people should be able to manage these things when they happen in our lives, if we manage them and deal with them in a proper manner we will be victorious but if we allow them to control our lives, we are going to live miserable lives. God is not pleased in seeing His people living miserable lives, but His wish is to see us being mature enough to handle the weapons that the enemy brings against us; these weapons are seen in the table below:

Debt	Discouragement
Delay	Disappointment
Dissension	Drowsiness

Debt

Debt is one of the areas in which the enemy watches in joy as people struggle day by day with their finances. The truth will remain the same regarding money, which is to say that money will never be enough regardlesss of what, it is your reponsibility as an individual to know how to manage your finances before it is too late. In life there are people who may seem to be seen as rich by others but yet they struggle with their finances. We should be very careful on how we spend our money. Latoya Irby gives us some reasons that teach us why debt is very bad for us, which are in the below points

Debt encourages you to spend more than you can afford: Debt ends up forcing us to use money in things that were not necessary. We end up buying things that were not stipulated in our monthly budgets, there are some instances such as auction sales, surprise parties and many more that end up leading us into borrowing money such that we also get to enjoy those kinds of thimngs, we should be careful of such and always make sure that we use our finances wisely.

Debt costs money: When we start borrowing money, most of the sources we borrow from demand an interest, this interest is costly and it may also affect our monthly budgets. It is better to save money than borrowing from someone else, we are living in a world that is full of issues that require money , sometimes we are stuck in situations that demand money right away so we end up borrowing money from others, the best way to be safe is to save some money for emergency situations.

Debt keeps you from reaching your financial goals: Most of the money that we try to save may be at times destroyed by the weapon called debt. In other words , debt takes us away from reaching our financial goals, because the money that we try to save for future goals ends up forcing us to use it in order to escape from debt. The best cure for this weapon called debt is to avoid living a life of debt by trying to be self-supporting and being self-sufficient. People who know how to keep money are never affected by debt because they know how dangerous the weapon called debt is, One of the favorite quotes by Emmanuel N Tshuma says ' We can not allow the weapon called debt to make our lives miserable yet this weapon has no brain and is not living'. It is better to run away from debt rather than making youself a slave to it.

Debt can lead to stress and serious medical problems: People who are in debt spend most of the time thinking on how they are going to pay back the money they owe. Things become even more tough if at all the money that you get is less than the debt that you have to pay, this brings strain and pain in the heart, life becomes miserable when situations like this arise. It is better to live a miserable life free from debt than living a miserable life with debt. Spending time thinking about debt, removes joy and peace in a person's heart, this may be also dangerous for health, because too much thinking can lead to depression, suicide , heart attacks and headaches which are harmful for our health. We must avoid debt at all costs.

Debt can hurt your marriage: There is nothing more painful than looking at a beautiful couple arguing over money. One day when Emmanuel N Tshuma was was taking a walk to the shops, when he reached there, he met a wonderful couple in the shop buying some groceries, it was during the month end and they were filling up the trolley with loads of groceries, whilst Emmanuel was watching them getting to the counter to pay for the groceries, suddenly the wife began to remind the husband about a certain ammount of money that they forgot that they had to pay, it looked like the money was more and they had to reduce the grocery that they had taken in the shop, the husband refused and said that they would borrow more money from one of his friends. The wife immediately shouted 'For how long are we going to live a life like this, a life full of debt , how are we going to survive like this with our children?' The couple began to be sad and they paid the groceries and left the shop. Emmanuel watched this whole incident with tears rolling down his eyes, it was indeed hurtful.

According to to Alyssa Girdwain on her teaching entitled '12 of the most common reasons for divorce, according to experts' , she mentions that one of the leading causes of divorce is financial issues, couples have to sit down together and talk on how they are going to use money rather than using money without agreeing with one another. (Girdwain, 2020)

Ecclesiastes 5:10 He who loves money will not be satisfied with money; nor he who loves wealth, with gain: this also is vanity. We must ask The Lord to help us stay away from debt because mney will never be enough.

Delay

The Merriam Webster dictionary defines delay as 'the act of postponing, hindering, or causing something to occur more slowly than normal. Delay can also be defined as 'to stop, detain, or hinder for a time. Delay is one of the areas in which the enemy works on in order to stop other important things being successful especially Christians. People who follow God are always at risk of being delayed by the enemy. We as Christians should be careful of such weapons. It is the plan of the enemy to cause distractions in many areas of our lives that can give us victory. Let us take a look at some of the top 3 delays that the enemy can brings in our lives:

The enemy can delay people in going to church. The church is the wife of Christ. It is a wonderful thing to go to church with the aim of praising and worshipping God with other brethren. The enemy is afraid of people who go to church because he knows that when they get there, the chances of collecting weapons like prayer and The Word of God as well as activating their spiritual lives are very high, so the enemy might cause obstacles like waking up late on a Sunday morning whilst planning to go to church or bringing illnesses that will eventually stop an individual going to church, we should be careful of such weapons, that is why it is a necessity to pray every morning when you wake up as well as praying in the evening before going to sleep.

The enemy can delay people from reaching their goals. One of the most sensitive areas we should be careful about is our vision, everyone has a vision that he/she wants to achieve in life. The enemy is aware of such things such that when he realizes that a certain individual might be close to being successful he can cause severe situations that are going to discourage that certain individual from being successful. There are some people in life that were so close to being successful for example, promotions at work, job opportunities, people willing to repent, but most of them have been delayed by the enemy such that they ended up ruining their targets. We need to constantly ask the Grace of The Lord to be with us always.

The enemy wants to delay people from knowing about God until death/Judgement day comes. There is no turning back when death comes, there is no repentance of sins after death. Repentance means the turning away from sin. There will be no turning back as well when Judgement day comes. The enemy has blinded the minds of the people on earth so that they think that Heaven and Hell are just mystery stories. The true story is that Heaven and Hell are real. It is better to repent for your sins now and live a right life required by God before it is too late. All of us are going to die one day but what matters is your personal relationship with God before you die, don't allow the enemy to use the weapon of delay in you.

Dissension

Webster's 1828 Dictionary (Webster, 1828)describes dissension as a disagreement in opinion, usually a disagreement which is violent, producing warm debates or angry words; contention in words; strife; discord; quarrel; breach of friendship and union.

The enemy becomes happy when he comes across churches which are quarrelling, families in strife, and relationships in argument. It is difficult to separate a couple that is always in peace as well as a church congregation that solves matters peacefully without any arguments. We should be careful with the way we handle ourselves when we are in arguments because the moment we become angry, that's the time when the enemy takes advantage and hinders us from getting the peace and harmony that is acceptable.

There are instances especially in churches and workplaces whereby leaders start arguing over a certain topic, people must learn to accept what is being said by the leaders, if the church leader or the executive manager says something that you might be against, it is better to try to advice peacefully without quarrelling, mocking and cursing because that is where the challenge comes.

Discouragement

At times we get discouraged in our workplaces, at home, at school and at the church; people hurt each other to a point whereby some victims end up being discouraged. People should learn to choose the words they say to others, it seems like the words we say to others end up hurting them to a point whereby they end up being even afraid to go to church. It is so painful to realise that some people never want to go back to church because they have been discouraged by other people. It is important to learn what to say and what not to say when you are around other people, of course fellowship is okay but if you end up talking something that is going to hurt another person, it becomes a challenge therefore we must learn to respect the boundaries of other people.

Most of the people especially at church have been discouraged so much such that they go to church just for the sake of going but deep down having that pain that is beyond in our hearts. It is wise to ask one another if we are alright or not, some people deserve support from us, but if we are going to do things on our own, going to church and leaving early before greeting others and asking them how they have been may be risky because you may never know what another person is going through. The enemy uses this weapon of discouragement to distract Christians so that they lose trust in God, so it is a must for us to be alert on these things and make sure that they do not only affect us but everyone around us.

Dissapointment

Disappointment is one of the weapons that the enemy uses to distract Christians. People most of the time get disappointed especially in churches. One of the main targets of the enemy is the church; the devil knows that church is powerful, so it is a serious threat to him. People get disappointed in church, for example when the pastor teaches on a certain topic during preaching time, one of the people can get disappointed thinking that the pastor is referring to him/her which is going to end up making her feel embarrassed and this can affect the way he/she attends church in the future.

Another instance can be whereby the pastor or church leader calls for members to come maybe for evangelism, cleaning or any activities in church only to realise that only few members show up for the event, this can cause disappointment to the church leader and might also bring pain as well. We as people should strive to cooperate together without leaving others to suffer whilst we are still available to help, of course at certain times we may be occupied but the little chance that you get you should make sure that you help in church activities. Some messages will always be hurtful but it is the role of our church leaders to correct us when we are wrong, when we refuse to be corrected, the consequences are going to backfire at us and cause more harm than in the first place. The truth shall set us free.

Drowsiness

Webster's 1828 dictionary defines drowsiness as sleepiness; heaviness with sleep; disposition to sleep. One of the main areas we should be careful about when we are at church is falling asleep especially when the Word is being preached. It is funny to look at how people sleep during services in most churches, when you fall asleep during a service or when The Word of God is taught just know that the enemy is using this weapon effectively in you. He does not want you to hear the message being delivered by the preacher, so sleeping is a way of distracting you from hearing the gospel.

Emmanuel N Tshuma has experienced drowsiness in the past years of his spiritual life, when he was in his teen years, Emmanuel used to sleep during preaching services and he would wake up just after the message was about to be concluded for the day, he came to realise that drowsiness is really a concern and we should avoid it at all costs and thank God he was delivered from that weapon before he became an adult.

It is better to rush to the toilet to go get a drink of water or carrying a water bottle at church, you can also stand up for a few minutes before sitting down just to get the mind prepared to listen to the Word of God, this weapon can be avoided from affecting us if we are zealous in hearing The Word of God. It will be also vital for us to teach the younger generation the correct posture that we should sit in church to avoid dosing during services so that this is transferred from generation to generation that will respect The Word of God and avoid sleeping during services at all costs.

Powerful Weapons That Should Be Used To Defeat The Enemy And His Team

Earlier in this book we discussed the weapons that are used by the enemy to distract Christians. The enemy's mission is to kill, steal and destroy everything that is in the world because he knows that his time is limited. Today I introduce to you the top 6 powerful weapons that Christians must use to defeat the enemy and his team. These weapons seem to be difficult to do but the end-results of them work 100% effectively. Every Christian who feels low, defeated by the enemy or who wants to grow spiritually should use these weapons to be successful in defeating the enemy. The weapons are as follows then we will explain them one by one so that we understand what they are all about. They are:

- **Prayer**
- **Fasting**
- **Reading The Word Of God**
- **Attending Church Services**
- **Living A Holy Life**
- **Having Faith**

Prayer

Prayer is the process of communicating with God. It is a way in which man link with God. Without prayer life becomes empty. Some people have not yet realised how powerful is but those who have felt and seen its power have committed them-selves to prayer and have made it a first priority in their lives. Most people pray even if they are not fully committed to God because during hard times, there is nothing that can save unless its prayer alone. Many miracles, blessings and wonders have happened through prayer, God is doing great and mighty things in the world today, people are getting healed through prayer, and people are receiving financial, material and spiritual blessings through prayer. It is one of the greatest weapons of spiritual warfare that are 100% effective, the spiritual opposition team which is the enemy is fearful of people who pray because they are very aware of its threat to them.

Stephen and Alek Kendrick in their book entitled 'The Battle Plan for Prayer' (Alex Kendrick and Stephen Kendrick, 2015) share with us the four types of prayer which are:

- Adoration: This is a prayer that praises and worships God. Sometimes as human beings, we have to learn to appreciate what The Lord has done for us. As people we have to learn to thank God for giving us an opportunity to live on earth, which on its own is a great blessing. If you are reading this book right now, you should consider yourself very blessed because millions in the world today are having a problem with their eyesight and some are blind. The book of Psalms 150 challenges us to praise God in whatever means because He is worthy to be praised and adored.

- Confession: This is a prayer that gets honest about sin. Living a right life which is not sinful is a requirement from God so it is necessary to confess our sins to God so that He might help us and give us an opportunity to be close to Him. The book of Isaiah 59:1 tells us that our iniquities have separated us and God even to a point that they have hid God's face from us. We must be never shy to confess our faults to God because no matter how bad people will think you are, as long as you talk to your God and He shall never leave nor forsake you.

- Thanksgiving: This is a God-directed, humbly expressed gratitude. Praise focuses on who God is, thanksgiving gives us a clear picture on what He has done or is doing in our lives. We as people should learn to give thanks to The Lord for He is good and worthy to be praised. We should be thankful for the blessings that The Lord has done in our lives, we should thank Him for giving us education, family, food, shelter and many other things, of course our blessings may be different from others but what we have to know is that everyone runs his/her own race. The Lord will reward you one day when your time comes.

- Supplication: This means requesting something from God. It means to beseech. Petition, or appeal for Him to do or provide something for ourselves and others. The book of James 4:2 tells us that we do not have things we wish for because we never ask. Some blessings are waiting for us to ask from God before they take place. We should learn that whatever we ask we will be given, whatever we seek, we shall find and when we knock on the door The Lord will be ready to open the door for us.

One of the most vital areas we should look at is the area of intercession; it carries the idea of intervening with a request on behalf of someone us. One of the greatest things that we can do is to intercede for others; this means praying as well for them so that God will make a way. Intercessors are the backbone of the church, they make sure that they always pray for others without judging or doing any means of harm but making sure that the grace of God is always sufficient.

God is our commander in chief in the spiritual, as we are fighting endless battles every day let us bear in mind that we will not achieve anything without prayer, we have to consistently yield to God and ask Him to help us fight our battles. The enemy is working 24/7 to make sure that he kills, steals and destroys, the power of prayer defeats his plans because where God is, there is always a way. We are conquerors through The Lord and we are nothing without Him. Several people who have tried defeating the enemy have failed because the enemy is also the commander of the evil forces; the truth is he has powers but his powers can only fail if God is involved.

The Bible talks about prayer and it deeply emphasizes us to continue praying the day The Lord will be coming for the second time. Prayer is a weapon that can be used at any time we just have to know and fully understand how powerful it is. Let us have a look on a few verses in The Bible that talk about Prayer.

1 Chorincles 16:11 Seek the LORD and his strength, seek his face continually.

Job 22:27 Thou shalt make thy prayer unto him, and he shall hear thee, and thou shalt pay thy vows.

James 5:16 Confess your faults one to another, and pray one for another, that ye may be healed. The effectual fervent prayer of a righteous man availeth much.

1 Thessalonians 5:17 Pray without ceasing.

Luke 11:1 And it came to pass, that, as he was praying in a certain place, when he ceased, one of his disciples said unto him, Lord, teach us to pray, as John also taught his disciples.

Let us make a habit to pray, of course it may seem hard and challenging in the beginning but as time goes on you will now learn until you are now spiritually mature even to appoint of teaching others. Jesus Christ taught His disciples how to pray, we must also teach our families and friends how to pray. In doing that they will realise how important and powerful prayer is until it is transferred from generation to generation.

A prayerful person makes a difference, at times we may seem to be discouraged on the way things are happening in this world, but the moment we surrender ourselves to God, things change, it is our responsibility to pray for pastors, wives, and friends, the community at large, governmental authorities over us, pastors, children and spouses. Doing this may enable a prayerful person to experience God in amazing ways.

The writer of this book Emmanuel N Tshuma has experienced the power of prayer from his junior years till his adult stage, God has been doing great and mighty things in front of him because of prayer, he saw the sick recovering right after prayer, he saw people getting jobs through prayer, he saw many people who were in spiritual bondage fully recovering and becoming free. We should never underestimate the power of prayer. The enemy will run away from people who are prayerful. The power of speaking in tongues enables a person to speak to God without the enemy hearing what is being talked about. May The Lord give us strength to overcome in this world by His help who is the creator and commander of the heavens and the earth.

Fasting

Fasting refers to self-denial of food for a couple of time giving oneself time for prayer and reading The Word of God until a time that will be planned. Fasting is one of the greatest essential weapons that should be used to defeat the devices of the enemy. It gives an individual time to concentrate only in the spiritual and be closer to God without being distracted by food and other things. Fasting can also be important for our health. Let us take a look at the benefits of fasting:

Physical Benefits According To Science

- Promotes blood sugar control by reducing insulin resistance

- Promotes better health by fighting inflammation

- May enhance heart health by improving blood pressure, Triglycerides and Cholesterol levels.

- May boost brain Function and prevent and prevent Nuero-degenerative disorders.

- Aids weight loss by limiting calorie intake and boosting metabolism.

- Could delay aging and extend long living.

- May aid in cancer prevention. (Link, 2018)

Spiritual Benefits Of Fasting

- Fasting creates an atmosphere that enables an individual to be closer to God.

- It helps a person to grow spiritually as it enables the self-denial of food making a person concentrate only in the spiritual leaving physical things behind.

- It helps a person to grow spiritually.

- It is used to break strongholds of the enemy.

- It creates an opportunity for an individual to concentrate on asking God on a specific need, having faith that God will answer and provide.

- Fasting gives us a clear picture to understand that spiritual warfare is real and we have to be aware of it.

- Fasting helps us to increase wisdom and knowledge regarding the Bible which is The Word of God.

Fasting is very important, in order for some things to happen, prayer must not be done alone, but fasting must be included in order to make a double-impact on the warfare category. Most common powerful weapons of today which are recognized today are prayer and fasting. Emmanuel N Tshuma classifies fasting in 5 categories which are:

Full-day fasting: This means from 0000 to 1800 Hrs, the individual does not eat anything for the whole day. The individual spends the day without eating even a small portion of food except water.

Full day dry fasting: This is whereby the individual does not eat anything from 0000 to 1800HRS including water. The individual spends most of the time thinking on spiritual things and uses his/her spare time at home, work or anywhere to pray and read The Word of God.

Half day fasting: The individual does not eat anything from 0000 to 1200 HRS, the individual only drinks water and spends the time connected in praying and studying the Bible. This kind of fasting may be beneficial and necessary for fasting beginners then with time they will slowly adjust until they are ready to fast for the whole day.

Half day dry fasting: The individual does not eat anything from 0000 to 1200 including water, he/she spends most of the time reading The Bible and prays often. This mode of fasting is beneficial for half day fasters to get used in fasting the whole day without eating anything. Half day fasting's in general can last up to 1500HRS even 1759 HRS.

Consecutive day fasting: This fasting lasts for more than one day , individuals spend most of time in The Word and in prayer, they only eat in the evening of the second or any other day they choose to seize the fasting at 1800HRS.

Consecutive day dry fasting: it is the same as the consecutive day fasting the only difference is that in this day; the individual goes for a couple of days without even drinking water.

Special fasting: This is whereby an individual chooses not to eat certain meals or food for a given period of time. For example someone may choose to drink only liquid food for the whole day without eating any other kind or vice versa. Special fasting can last up to a long time.

Fasting is always good and it never disappoints. Most of the people who took time fasting have received blessings and they have seen their needs being answered. Let us take a look at a couple of verses that talk about fasting in The Bible.

Exodus 34:28 and he was there with the LORD forty days and forty nights; he did neither eat bread, nor drink water. And he wrote upon the tables the words of the covenant, the Ten Commandments.

Ezra 10:6 Then Ezra rose up from before the house of God, and went into the chamber of Johanan the son of Eliashib: and when he came thither, he did eat no bread, nor drink water: for he mourned because of the transgression of them that had been carried away.

Mark 2:19 and Jesus said unto them, can the children of the bridechamber fast, while the bridegroom is with them? As long as they have the bridegroom with them, they cannot fast.

Matthew 4:2 and when he had fasted forty days and forty nights, he was afterward an hungred.

Psalms 35:13 but as for me, when they were sick, my clothing was sackcloth: I humbled my soul with fasting; and my prayer returned into mine.

Fasting is beneficial in our lives, when we do it, God will bless us more and more and we will receive spiritual breakthrough and see things moving in ways that we want. Fasting makes the enemy to be embarrassed because he knows that it is so powerful.

Reading The Word Of God

In the beginning was The Word and The Word was with God and The Word was God. The Word of God is found in The Bible. The Bible is a powerful weapon that is used to defeat the enemy. The Bible was written by 40 different authors inspired by God. We must stick to The Bible and learn a lot from eat, the more we read it is the more we gain wisdom and knowledge that we must use to understand the tactics of the enemy and establish motives on how to defeat the plans. Below is a table of some Bible Statistics taken from the internet, it gives us a summary on what The Bible is all about: (Hunter, 2013)

Number of books in The Bible= 66	Books of Genesis to Deuteronomy written by Moses
Chapters in the Bible= 1189	Number of translated languages=1200
Verses in The Bible= 31 101	Number of time the word The Lord appears= 7736
Words in The Bible= 783 137	Shortest verses= John 11:35
Commands=6468	Longest verses= Esther 8:9
Fulfilled prophecy= 3268	Middle books= Micah and Nuham
Longest chapter= Psalms 119	Longest name= Mahershalahashbaz
Shortest chapter= Psalms 117	Number of promises given=1260

The Word of God is pure and holy, everything written in The Bible is what God wanted us to know and understand more. Let us not underestimate the Bible and let us follow what God wants us to do in this earth, we came here for a purpose and we should make sure we achieve our mission by reading The Word of God always and following what it says. Let us take a look at a couple of verses in the Bible that show us how important it is to read The Word of God:

Luke 11:28 and he said, `Yea, rather, happy those hearing the word of God, and keeping it!'

Acts 6:4 and we to prayer, and to the ministration of the word, will give ourselves continually.'

2 Corinthians 5:19 how that God was in Christ--a world reconciling to Himself, not reckoning to them their trespasses; and having put in us the word of the reconciliation.

Hebrews 4:12 For the word of God is quick, and powerful, and sharper than any two-edged sword, piercing even to the dividing asunder of soul and spirit, and of the joints and marrow, and is a discerner of the thoughts and intents of the heart. (KJV)

The Word of God is powerful. It was powerful in the past, still powerful in this present time and it will always be powerful until the second coming of The Lord, he who follows the bible shall never be harassed by the enemy, he who reads the Bible shall gain more wisdom and understanding, he who talks to others about The Word of God shall be blessed. Let us use this weapon to disarm the weapons of the enemy that has been set upon us. The Word of God is powerful!

Attending Church Services

Attending church services is one of the most important things that we should do as people in this world. The church is the area in which people come together to worship and praise God as well as sharing The Word of God with each other; people get revived through church services. We are in a spiritual world war and the devil is fighting each and every day to distract people in the world. Going to church enables people to release on big weapon like a nuclear bomb which is going to defeat the plans of the enemy. The devil is afraid of a church service because he knows that it is an area where people activate their spiritual weapons to defeat him. Rhonda Stoppe gives us some reasons that encourage us why we should attend church services:

To hear the preaching of The Word: When we attend church services, we get an opportunity to learn The Word of God, and by doing this, we become motivated and encouraged in our lives. The Word of God is so powerful such that it can heal, inspire, rebuke, motivate and correct. We need the Word of God in our spiritual lives daily.

Participating in praise and worship: We attend church services to worship The Lord and praise Him, giving Him thanks for He is good and His mercy endures forever. When we worship, we inspire others to connect as well and follow what is being done. Church gives an opportunity to grow mightily spiritually.

Iron sharpens iron: There is a saying that says 'iron sharpens iron' which means that a Christian can only sharpen another Christian. No Christian can be sharpened in the world outside church because we live in an era where the world is become more polluted by the devices of the enemy, the safest way is to go to church and mend ways with God.

Exercising gifts: There are many people who would have been far right now if at all they attended church services to feel the power of God. Attending church services helps us as individuals to realise certain spiritual gifts that God has given. One man by the name of Emmanuel Tshuma did not know that he would be a professional drummer and a teacher of The Word in the past when he was new in the church, as time went by still attending church he realised that he could play drums, later on after a couple of years he moved to the keyboard and later on again learned the bass guitar. As time went by Emmanuel began to realise that he had a good ability to teach, he went to Bible school and later finished. All these gifts took place because of attending church services.

To encourage the church leader: Churches of today have bishops, pastors, evangelists, prophets, apostles and teachers. All of them require support from saints, attending church services encourages them as well to move forward and carry on mentoring and encouraging their saints at all times. The book of Philippians 1:3-7 tells of Apostle Paul. His affection for these precious people who partnered with him in spreading the glorious gospel of grace. In the same way, when we become a partner in ministry with our church leaders we bring joy in their hearts, we encourage them to keep on praying for us always and appreciating the wonderful support that we give them always.

To find godly mentors: The church has many people who have lived challenging lives and have passed through many obstacles that may be very important to teach us so that we learn from them. Having a godly mentor means that you will always have someone who looks on you,

guides and encourages you on the paths you take and always making sure that you always receive the support that you need. God values mentorship. The book of Titus 2 deeply teaches us the importance of mentorship. When we mentor each other it will be difficult for us to fall into sin, we therefore need each other as brothers and sisters in Christ, working together in living lives that will make The Lord proud.

To teach kids: We are living in a world that has many people who still do not know about God. It is painful to realise that people do not understand what is being meant by spirituality. Teaching kids whilst they are still young will help fight this problem. When a child grows up in The Lord it doesn't become easy for him/her to forget about God when reaching adult stage. The world would be a better place if at all people understood spiritual life. It is our duty as human beings to teach the young generation about God so that in the future they will carry on the legacy until the second coming of The Lord.

To be a light to the community: A lot of people watch and observe those who go to church, the world is in darkness, it needs people who have the light so that they show the way that should be followed to others. The community must never be discouraged in going to church because of the mistakes and problems that we do; instead the community should be inspired to go to church through us.

To carry each other's burdens: The book of Galatians 6:2 says 'Bear one another's burdens, and so fulfil the law of Christ'. Hebrews

12:1 continues to says 'Wherefore seeing we also are compassed about with so great a cloud of witnesses, let us lay aside every weight, and the sin which doth so easily beset us, and let us run with patience the race that is set before us'. It is our role to carry one another's burdens not only in church but outside as well, carrying each other's burdens destroys some bad things for example gossip, depression, tale-bearing, cursing and all others, carrying each other's burdens contributes to a successful church that is full of unity, respect and love.

Because God says so: God requires us to attend church. The book of Hebrews 10:25 says 'not forsaking the assembling of ourselves together, as the manner of some is; but exhorting one another: and so much the more, as ye see the day approaching'. God desires us to attend church regularly so that we try by all means to be revived because the hard days are approaching; the only one who can save us in this difficult time is God. Let us make it a habit of going to church always. There is nothing like 'I will worship God on my own at home'. Saying this is like a soldier saying to 'I will fight on my own during war', it is impossible to fight the enemy alone, we need each other as brethren to work together in fighting the enemy, he is also strong, we must never underestimate him but all we should know is that with God by our side we are victorious and nothing can hinder us.

Living A Holy Life

Living a holy life is a powerful weapon on its own; the enemy plays far from people who are holy because he knows that he can never trick them and his team. Living a holy life has never been easy and it will never be easy until the day The Lord returns to earth. It is easy to fall into sin but it is difficult to stay away from sin. Living a holy life requires a person who is committed; this means that a committed person will stick on his/her plans without letting anything interfere with his/her plans.

God requires everyone to live holy lives. This is a life that is required by God. A life that is not sinful. It is a life that sticks in living the way that God wants. Unfortunately we are living in a world that is being covered by lies, gossiping, slander, tale-bearing, sexual immorality, killings, etc. That on its own is a challenge. The book of John 10:10 teaches us that the enemy has come to steal, kill and destroy. The Lord requires us to be careful of the enemy always and run away from sin and other sinful acts. Below are some points that will help us use the weapon of living a holy life effectively.

- Repenting our sins daily and asking God to forgive us.

- Following what the book of Acts 2:38 says about living a holy life

- Displaying positive character at work, school and the community at large

- Solving issues peacefully at work, school and the community at large.

- Avoiding fighting and arguments with other people

- Forgiving others

- Learning to be content with what you have

- Wearing modest apparel when going to shops, weddings or any other place

- Praying daily

- Running away from sinful acts.

- Encouraging others to trust and believe in God

- Spreading the gospel to each and every person just like the book of Matthew 28:19 says.

All these powerful points create a powerful weapon we call ' Living a holy life' we should shame the devil and show him that living a holy life is possible, he may try by all means to distract our lives but let us always bear in mind that God is there for us every time. May The Good Lord help us to live holy lives so that we become examples in this world to others who think that living a holy life is impossible.

Having Faith

Hebrews 11:1 makes it clear that faith is the substance of things hoped for, the evidence of things not seen. Many people have experienced the power of faith in their lives starting from the many different stories in The Bible. When we begin to see things happening trusting and having faith in our Lord, that's when we will begin to see and understand how powerful our God is. Let us have a look on different verses in the Bible that talk about faith:

Psalms 37:5 Commit thy way unto the LORD; trust also in him; and he shall bring it to pass.

Matthew 9:29 Then touched he their eyes, saying, According to your faith be it unto you

Matthew 17:20 And Jesus said unto them, Because of your unbelief: for verily I say unto you, If ye have faith as a grain of mustard seed, ye shall say unto this mountain, Remove hence to yonder place; and it shall remove; and nothing shall be impossible unto you.

Luke 8:25 and he said unto them, Where is your faith? And they being afraid wondered, saying one to another, What manner of man is this! for he commandeth even the winds and water, and they obey him.

James 5:15 And the prayer of faith shall save the sick, and the Lord shall raise him up; and if he have committed sins, they shall be forgiven him.

Faith heals the sick: When people who are sick trust in God and believe that when the believers lay their hands upon them they will recover, they get healed instantly. The book of Matthew 10:1 tells us that when Jesus called forth the twelve apostles, he gave them the power to heal all manner of sickness and disease. The good news is that we are the chosen apostles of today, when we have faith in God , we will pray for the sick and they will get healed, what is important is for them to also have faith in God believing that God can do the impossible.

Faith can bring jobs: There are many people who got jobs through faith and trust in The Lord. Our God will not disappoint those who lay their trust upon Him. One of the people who can testify of how faith is important is the writer of this book Emmanuel N Tshuma, he saw the way faith is powerful, few years ago whilst he applied for a job, he was called for an interview that lasted for more than a month, he used to go there almost every day, it was very difficult for him. He had some obstacles that he felt will disqualify him from getting that job, one good morning he sat down and began thinking of how powerful his God is, he decided to make Hebrews 11:1 his daily inspiration, he was one of the thousands that were called for the interview, it was rough and challenging during the selection process but Emmanuel is happy to testify that he became one of the few hundreds that were selected for the job. He used to kneel down and prayer each morning before going for the interview until he became successful. This is an illustration of how powerful our God is when we trust in Him, no situation is hard for The Lord.

Faith can build stronger friendships, relationships and marriages: Friends and couples who constantly pray for their friendships and relationships to be strong and last for ever never go wrong in that, there are many friendships and marriages today that have lasted for a longer period of time and are still even more strong, this is because the two parties agreed with each other that no matter how challenges and situations may affect them they will always be strong by correcting each other's mistakes and seeking The Lord for help. Having faith in God will always leave you with a smile on your face because The Lord God never disappoints.

Stubborn faith is necessary: Sometimes we have to use stubborn faith because it is necessary. The book of Matthew 17:20 says ' And Jesus said unto them, Because of your unbelief: for verily I say unto you, If ye have faith as a grain of mustard seed, ye shall say unto this mountain, Remove hence to yonder place; and it shall remove; and nothing shall be impossible unto you'. Miracles and wonders have happened to those who had stubborn faith, regardless of the situation that haunted them they still had faith in God and believed that He could do miracles and wonders. These situations have happened, they are actually happening and they will always happen even in the future, we are talking of situations whereby we see praying for the sick then all of a sudden they get healed instantly, praying for the dead to come back to life, or any other situation which may seem too hard but being possible through fearless trust in The Lord our God who created the Heaven and the earth.

Faith gives us protection from God. All people who lay their trust on The Lord as well as believing that God will always be there for them wherever they go whatever they do, who they meet, what they eat, who they work with as well as who they fellowship with, will always receive protection from The Lord , the powers and principalities of the enemy never work in people who have strong faith in God, only the weak ones are defeated by the enemy, it is the wish of God to see His people laying their trust on Him because He will always be there for them. He is the same yesterday, today and forever.

A Glimpse of Spiritual World War

We are living in a physical world; history confirms that in the past World War I and World War II took place. World War I began on 28 July 1914 and lasted until 11 November 1918. More than 9 million combatants and 7 million civilians died as a result of the war. On the other hand World War II began on 1939 and lasted until 1945; it involved 100 million people from over 30 countries. Marked by the mass deaths of civilians, including the holocaust(during which approximately 11 million people were killed) and the strategic bombing of industrial and population centres (during which approximately one million people were killed, including the use of two nuclear weapons in combat) It resulted in an estimated 50 million to 85 million fatalities. This made world war II the greatest conflict in human history.

World war happened in the world and that was in the physical, today if at all you did not know, we are in a spiritual world war that is around the whole of this world and is everywhere. Spiritual world war is real and we must know that is exists.

Spiritual World War = started before men were created, the book of Revelation 12: 7 tells us about it which says:

Revelation 12:7 and there was war in heaven: Michael and his angels fought against the dragon; and the dragon fought and his angels.

Spiritual world war took place in Heaven, Michael and his angels were fighting against the dragon who was the enemy himself, also called the devil, before he was called the devil, his name was Lucifer and he was the most respected and high ranking angels in Heaven, unfortunately he turned his back and started challenging God which ended up causing havoc in heaven, during that time he had already influenced some angels in Heaven who chose to follow him. This led to him being cast into the earth with his team; we see the confirmation of this in the book of Revelation 12: 9 which goes on to say:

Revelation 12:9 and the great dragon was cast out, that old serpent, called the Devil, and Satan, which deceiveth the whole world: he was cast out into the earth, and his angels were cast out with him.

The enemy has made himself the god of this world because he views himself in charge of everything. His mission is to confuse people in the world by leading them astray so that when judgement comes, he takes many people with him. Spiritual world war is going to last until the second coming of The Lord. It long began since the time of Adam and Even when they ate the forbidden fruit, it continued at Sodom and Gomora, passed in the time when Christ died on the cross for our sins and it will also continue until the day of judgement. It is time to be spiritually aware of this world war because it is happening even now as we speak, the enemy and his team are at work, God and His angels are also at work at this present moment, God has given us the opportunity to choose where we want to belong because there are only two groups that are involved in this spiritual world war, the team of God and the team of Satan. Below is a table that tries to explain all about this spiritual world war.

Diagram of Spiritual War Zone

GOD'S TEAM	SATAN'S TEAM
Apostles, prophets, evangelists, pastors and teachers	Fake Christians who act like true Christians
Good morals	Bad morals
Eternal life	Burning fire
The Bible	Unacceptance of The Bible
Belief	Unbelief
Good angels	Bad angels

Prayer	Lives without prayer
Fasting	Temporary pleasure
Love	Hate
Happiness	Unhappiness
Unity	Gossip
Care	Hypocritical people
Faithfulness	Unfaithfulness
Peace and harmony	Arguments and fights
Intercessors	Spiritual wickedness in high places and the rulers of the darkness of the world
The Holy Spirit	Possession
Deliverance	Initiation
Spiritual awareness	Spiritually blind
Attending church services	Never going to church

Spiritual warzone is real and is happening in the spiritual, there are different spirits found around the area that we live in, and those spirits only come from two categories. Other spirits belong to God whilst the others belong to Satan. The best plan is to be spiritually awake and to be spiritually alert at all times. Those that belong to the enemy are temporary, one day they are going to fade but believing and following God is eternal. The enemy has placed his team in different areas across the world, he has even placed some in the church, and this means we now have to be more careful than ever, they come in sheep's clothing at church but deep down being wolves that have come to kill, steal and destroy. The enemy's team can also perform miracles and wonders that are the same as the one's done by God, people must have those spiritual mature eyes that can detect that something is not right. This is only achieved through commitment, prayer, fasting and consistently reading The Word of God. When we do that we will begin to realise that the enemy is not really someone to be scared of, he distracts those that are still in darkness without knowledge. The enemy is afraid of people who are fully committed to God because he knows that he cannot tempt them in any way. A good example is Job in The Bible, he lost everything but never gave up on God, and we need people like Job in this present time that cannot be shaken by anything including the powers and destructions of the enemy.

Spiritual World War To End After Rapture

Just like mentioned earlier in the beginning of the book, when we talk about the things Of God, we talk about serious business, there are no jokes here, when you see Christians going house to house preaching The Word they are not wasting their time but they are doing the people who have not yet known about God a favour by telling them to prepare whilst there is still time. The sad part of spiritual warzone is that all those who are in the opposition team that is the team of the devil will end up in the lake of fire during judgement, prepare for the second coming of The Lord. Let us look at a dream that Emmanuel had one night on the year 2021.

Emmanuel was in a big city full of people, he was one of the respected people and one of the wealthiest people who lived in the richest people. As he looked he could see that he was living in a big flat, there were many flats joined together and it looked as if he was staying in the same area with some work employees. It happened that one day, Emmanuel and the rest of the employees in the company were called in a big meeting by their boss and were told to gather in a big room, to discuss some business ideas on how to save the economy because it looked like life was getting rough and rough. There seemed to be a shortage of resources, petrol, food and oil were beginning to be hard to find. The world was running out of resources.

Suddenly during the midst of their meeting, the sky became dark, a white cloud began to show itself in the midst of the black atmosphere, they began to see a big cross, the cross became bigger and bigger until they eventually saw angels with wings descending, the colours as Emmanuel remembered were orange and red, many angels started descending from the sky, in the midst of them was one angel that Emmanuel couldn't tell who it was. At that same moment, people started screaming, the world panicked, shops were open, buildings were opened, cars stopped moving, people in hospitals came out to see what was happening. People started finding ways to escape. Soldiers, policemen and others of the law started to run away, as Emmanuel could see, there was no use in escaping because the numbers of the angels in the sky were more than the people in the location.

After moments of panic and fear, the area that Emmanuel was located only had a few people left who were viewing in the sky, Emmanuel started forcing his way through the crowd until eventually he could view the angels who were now standing on the ground. Emmanuel immediately started pointing at one of the angels and started praying. 'God you are the only one who can save us, you are the King of Kings the Lord of Lords'. Suddenly after that prayer, the angel that Emmanuel pointed, started smiling and immediately afterwards, some people started vanishing whilst others were left, and people who were left cried bitterly. There was destruction everywhere. Before more things were seen, Emmanuel saw himself being removed from the area that he was located in until he could not see anyone anymore.

Rapture is real and is coming, it is time for people to realise that whilst there is still time because one day, that opportunity will expire and it will be too late to repent and ask God for forgiveness. It is better for everyone to make sure that they mend their relationship with God. Let us take a look on a couple of verses that talk about the rapture in the Bible:

Genesis 28:12 And he dreamed that there was a ladder set up on the earth, and the top of it reached to heaven; and behold, the angels of God were ascending and descending on it!

Psalms 40:16 but May all who seek thee rejoice and be glad in thee; may those who love thy salvation say continually, "Great is the LORD!"

2 Timothy 3:1 but understand this that in the last days there will come times of stress.

Proverbs 15:16 Better is a little with the fear of the LORD than great treasure and trouble with it.

Matthew 6:19-20 "Do not lay up for yourselves treasures on earth, where moth and rust consume and where thieves break in and steal, but lay up for yourselves treasures in heaven, where neither moth nor rust consumes and where thieves do not break in and steal."

The Bible has said it all, we must prepare for the second coming of The Lord, we are soldiers in the Lord's army. God is our commander and we have spiritual leaders like church leaders and bishops who will always encourage us spiritually and groom us in the way that The Lord desires. The second coming of Christ is real, rapture is real and is coming, others will be dead, others will be alive but the truth is that everyone will experience that and see it happening in real life.

If at all there are people who still doubt on the existence of The Lord, they should re-consider their thoughts and re-think again. The mission of Christians today is to also recruit new members from the world who do not know about God. Through various lessons, teaching, prayer and reading The Word of God, they will begin to understand the things of the spiritual so that they also find groom new soldiers in the Kingdom of God. It seems like soldiers are limited, if at all you are not yet born again it is time to sit down and think about this, because everything talked about in this book is real. If at all you are reading this book and you are already a born-again Christian, it is time to revive your spiritual life and pray more, read The Bible more and be more spiritually alert. Some people think that things of the spiritual are a joke; some say it's been long since Christians said The Lord will come back till now. The answer to that question is, we do not know the day of the coming of The Lord, when the day comes it will be difficult to repent because time is going to stop, it is better to use the little opportunity that you have before it is too late, you do not have to wait until the next day to turn your life around and live a new life. What if tomorrow never comes? Rapture is real. Let the gospel be taught unto all nations. Those who will accept will accept and those who will reject will reject, but the truth remains the same, the day is coming whereby the earth will come to an end.

Spiritual Soldiers Wanted

God, the creator of the universe, the Commander of all principality and power is looking for spiritual soldiers who are ready to defend the Word of God and keep the good fight of faith. This spiritual war is real and people who have not yet known about God must know him before it gets too late. There are man of God, Christian elders and many others who are there to equip those who are still new with the Word so that they may also grow spiritually and teach the future generations to come. Like in the military, spiritual camps are available everywhere. The church is a good example of a spiritual camp. This is whereby spiritual soldiers, being Christians meet and get basic instructions on how to fight the devices of the enemy seen in the world today.

Our workplaces, community, home and school is our battleground. This is our warzone and this is whereby we meet different types of spiritual things that challenge our spiritual lives. We as spiritual soldiers should be always ready to fight at any time. If we are weak, the enemy will defeat us because he is very deadly and he knows that he needs every opportunity he gets to divert Christian soldiers into his soldiers. A soldier is always ready to fight at any time. A spiritual soldier should be as well ready to fight any time. For example if a Christian soldier is at work and he/she begins to realise that the environment is heavy spiritually, he/she must cast away the burden and begin praying, if someone is sick, spiritual soldiers should pray that person , because the Bible says greater is He in you than the one in the world.

Let us take a look at what the book of Matthew 10:1 and Luke 9:1 teaches.

Matthew 10:1 And when he had called unto him his twelve disciples, he gave them power against unclean spirits, to cast them out, and to heal all manner of sickness and all manner of disease.

Luke 9:1 Then he called his twelve disciples together, and gave them power and authority over all devils, and to cure diseases.

We are the chosen apostles of today; God has given us the ability to pray for one another so that we get healed. Spiritual soldiers are always ready for anything at any time. As spiritual soldiers we should also know that it is our responsibility to also recruit new soldiers as well in the army of God, soldiers who are going to learn to fight the enemy and his team when we leave earth, because we are not going to live for ever in this world, there is going to come a time whereby we will be no more qualified to live on this earth. Therefore it is wise for us to teach the younger generation and as well train the upcoming spiritual soldiers so that they will carry on the work of God even when we are not around. The Bible teaches us to preach and teach the gospel to other souls on this earth, let us take a look at a few verses below that talk about spreading the Word.

Proverbs 11:30 the fruit of the righteous is a tree of life; and he that winneth souls is wise.

Proverbs 14:25 a true witness delivereth souls: but a deceitful witness speaketh lies.

Isaiah 52:7 How beautiful upon the mountains are the feet of him that bringeth good tidings, that publisheth peace; that bringeth good tidings of good, that publisheth salvation; that saith unto Zion, Thy God reigneth.

Mark 13:10 and the gospel must first be published among all nations.

God, our commander has given all of His soldiers an order that should be done by all spiritual soldiers of all ranks starting with the senior bishops until it reaches the new spiritual soldier. That order is 'to deliver the word to each and every creature in the earth'. Soldiers take orders without disputing, therefore as spiritual soldiers we are to take this order seriously, and The Bible has even told us that there is joy in heaven over one sinner that repents. We are short of spiritual soldiers in the army of God; we need more strength in this world because the commander of the opposition team (Satan) is also fighting to recruit more soldiers in his army. We should be more extra careful of the opposition team. The book of **2Timothy 3:1** says **'This know also, that in the last days perilous times shall come.'** Unfortunately we are living in a time whereby Satan's soldiers wear the same uniform as the soldiers of God, these so called soldiers are claiming to be part of

God's team on the outside, but deep inside they are wolves in sheeps clothing, the Bible clearly warns us about such people. We are taught that we shall see them by their works that they are not true soldiers of the army of The Lord.

The Lord has given us different spiritual weapons to fight the enemy; these weapons should always be there close to you, because if they are far, the enemy will take advantage and distract you. Some of the major weapons are prayer, fasting, reading the Word of God, living a holy life, having faith and attending church, with these 6 major weapons, you will not go wrong in life in your spiritual walk. May the good Lord help us to fight and keep on moving forward until the time comes where we will receive our reward in Heaven.

Summary

In the beginning of this book, we realise that this world is in spiritual battle. It seems like there is a battle between right and wrong, good and bad. This is whereby several positions of the church were taken in order of the top to the last category, these spiritual categories show and teach us the importance of leadership during a battle, a team that wins is a team that takes orders as they are and implements them without disputing or quarrelling. We were taken to the spiritual categories which taught us about God as our commander, under God we saw the three high rank angels followed by other angels. These positions were explained in military style so that people could understand more and better on what is really meant by spiritual leadership. For example at the highest ranking of the military, the commander is in charge whereas in the spiritual, God is the commander; the angels are classified as major generals and brigadiers.

The various positions were taken from the country leaders, church leaders, church elders, ministry department leaders, church attenders and new church attenders. In the military when someone is new and wants to be a soldier, he or she is first taken for military training whereby he/she will be taught on how to use weapons and survive during war as well as doing all military duties. The same way happens in a new church attender, various church denominations have different ways in which they teach, mould and establish spiritual soldiers in the army of God who are ready to serve Him with their whole hearts and live for Him. New church attenders who are willing to be committed are taught different lessons that will help them realise and learn about spiritual warzone so that they are aware of the weapons of the enemy and as well find ways in which they could do to defeat the enemy and his team, one of the ways in doing this is by prayer and fasting. Spiritual war zone is real and spiritual soldiers are needed to fight their best by making sure the name of The Lord is preached and taught on all nations so that people can understand about the spiritual on how it is real and existing. The book of John 10:10 teaches us that the enemy has not only come to this earth but to kill, steal and destroy, we as Christians have to work together in defeating this enemy because the enemy is also fighting to distract the people on earth before the second coming of The Lord, this leads to us having a brief teaching concerning spiritual warzone.

Spiritual Warzone is real. It is the main focus in this book, the enemy who is the devil is fighting left and right, his mission is to kill, steal and destroy those who want to follow God, some of the physical weapons that the enemy uses on people is diseases, war, technology, arguments, pride of life, corruption, inequality, discrimination, miserable lives, sexual immorality, revenge, love of money, abuse, stealing and unplanned events. The enemy has spiritual weapons as well that he uses to distract Christians, there are the ten deadly sins that are committed by the mouth which are lying, cursing, slander, tale-bearing, sowing discord, cursing, filthy language, blasphemy, contentious speech and unbelief. There are also spiritual weapons that the enemy uses like anger, laziness, discontentment, lust depression, jealousy, hatred, un-forgiveness, backsliding and selfishness.

Powerful weapons that are used to defeat the enemy and his team include prayer, fasting, reading the Word of God, living a holy life and attending church services. The enemy is working day and night, therefore we must be alert always and be ready to fight him, we cannot fight him alone, we need God by our side because God is the creator of the universe and nothing is impossible with Him. Let us take a look at the story below which shows how dangerous the enemy is. It was a testimony of Prophet Aston Adam Mbaya about the 351 chambers of Hell.

The Battle And War Against Churches And Pastors

So Lucifer entrusted me with the mission to fight the pastor of a Church in my country Congo-Brazza. When I arrived in the city of Pointe Noire where the church was, I began by investigating the pastor. After this investigation, I finally discovered his strength.

I discovered that he was a man who feared God and who was powerful in prayer. The implication of all this was disturbing. In fact, it prevented our movements and activities in the city. In his church, there was an intercession group that prayed every day and every night. Beloved you must understand that the enemy does not attach hypocritical Christians because they belong to him. Only those who walk in holiness and the fear of The Lord will draw the attention of the devil.

This pastor was a member of a community of many churches, but he was the one who feared God. That is why the devil designated him as a potential target. My strategy against this pastor was to extinguish the fire that shone and burned in him. My tactic was to get him break the law so that I could have access to his life. I was also supposed to stop his evangelical journey to Europe. Whenever he went to the administrative offices for the visa, I deployed demons in those offices to oppose him, but the main purpose was to make sure that this pastor could break the law. I had 800 warrior demons working against this pastor. Failure in the kingdom of darkness is unacceptable. So we worked hard. But despite our determination, this pastor was constant and intense in prayer. So I summoned the chief sorcerer of this neighbourhood and his brotherhood so that he could go to this pastor and complain about the noises caused by the intercessors in their prayers. In fact, in all quarters of the world, a chief or secretary general of sorcerers has been established. I told the chief sorcerer, 'Gather all the sorcerers in this area and go to the pastor, you must pretend that the intercessors make noise with their prayers at night and people cannot sleep'. So in the morning, the sorcerers went to see the pastor to complain. They approached this pastor with abusive and shocking language to make him feel offended. It was a powerful strategy that succeeded because the pastor reacted with pride. As a result a door in his life was opened and the sorcerers managed to send a demon into the life of this pastor through the door of pride. He was spiritually weak and his attempt to travel to Europe failed. You must understand that the devil will seek an open door to access your life. Anger and offense are the two great main doors used by sorcerers against the children of God. The Bible says 'Be angry but do not sin; do not let the sun go down on your anger. Ephesians 4:26. I managed to extinguish the fire of this man of God.'

It is time to re-think about our spiritual lives and begin to work on our weaknesses, everyone has a weakness and the sad part is that the enemy will use the weakness as a gateway to deploy his demons into your life, the best way to escape from this is to be prayerful, we must repent our sins always, we must follow what the book of Acts 2:38 says, by being born again and leaving our past life into a new life that is required by God. It is time to preach The Word of God without fail it is time to go house to house preaching and teaching people about The Lord. For the days have become evil, people lose their lives every day through passion killings, illnesses, accidents and other causes, the danger part is that every one of us does not know when he/she is going to die. It is painful to die without giving your life to God; it is risky to live a life that is not of God because you never know what might happen tomorrow. This book has taken us through various areas in which the devil operates, on order to be victorious, we have to learn first on our surroundings as well as planning and thinking of strategies and tactics that will help us be aware of the weapons used by the enemy. The devil knows that he is already defeated by God and that he will be chased to the lake of fire during Judgement day.

The day is coming whereby everything on earth will stop, the day is approaching whereby everyone will be judged according to his/her deeds, it may seem funny to see people going to church every day and living holy lives, even though some of them are hypocritical, there are some who are fearful of The Lord and God is going to bless such people more and more. We have to allow the Bible to give us wisdom and knowledge, by doing that we end up having a wide understanding on the devil and his tactics and by that we end up destroying his mission through the power of God. The Lord has not created us to be defeated in this world, but He gave us an opportunity to have freewill and be victorious. May The Lord bless us in each and every area of our lives. May God give us the strength to overcome the weapons of the enemy so that we can trust and be strong without having the fear of being defeated? May The Lord help us to be strong enough to live lives that are going to qualify us to escape the lake of fire and go to heaven where there will be eternal joy. Amen

References

Most of the scripture quotations are taken from the Revised Standard Version and the King James Version of the Bible.

All scriptures in this entire book taken from the BibleCD (Online Publishing, Inc, 2010)

Bibliography

Churchpop. (2019, 10 06). The powerful meanings behind The three Archangels' Names, in One Amazing Infographic. Retrieved 03 01, 2021, from www.churchpop.com: www.churchpop/2019/10/06/thepowerful-meanings-behind-the-3-archangels-names-in-one-amazing-infographic/amp/

Girdwain, A. (2020, 04 14). 12 Of The Most Common Reasons For Divorce,

According To The Experts. Retrieved 03 06, 2021, from womenshealthmag.com: www.womenshealthmag.com/relationships/a32019433/reasons-for-divorce/

Grudem, W. (2017, 12 13). Angels in the Bible: What do we actually know about them. Retrieved 03 02, 2021, from zondervanacademic.com: zondervanacademic.com/blog/biblical-facts-angels

Hayden, J. B. (2016, 09 05). Famous People Who Mocked God and Met Their Untimely Death. Retrieved 03 12, 2021, from HearSayGhblog.wordpress.com: www.google.com/amp/s/hearsayghblog.wordpress.com/2016/09/05/famous-people-who-mocked-god-and-met-their-untimely-death/amp/

Herring, H. (not specified, not specified not specified). The Seven Favorite Weapons Of Satan. Retrieved 03 06, 2021, from haroldherring.com: haroldherring.com/blogs/harolds-blogs/richthoughts/827-the-seven-favorite-weapons-of-satan

History of The World. (2016, 01 10). World War II. Bandar Jengka, Taman Permatang Shahbander, Malaysia.

History.com editors. (2019, 09 21). Satanism. Retrieved 03 03, 2021, from History.com: www.google.com/.amp/topics/1960s/satanism

Hunter, M. (2013, 04 29). Amazing Bible Timelinewith World History. Retrieved 03 03, 2021, from amazingbibletimeline.com: amazingbibletimeline.com/blog/q10_bible_facts_statistics/

Insta encouragements. (2018, 02 11). 16 Nmes of God and What They Mean.

Retrieved 03 12, 2021, from instaencouragements.com: www.instaencouragements.com/blog/16-names-of-god-and-what-they-mean

Irby, L. (2020, 09 29). 9 Reasons Debt is Bad for You. Retrieved 03 06, 2021, from thebalance.com: www.thebalance.com/reasons-debt-is-bad-960048

Kroll, W. (2012). A study from the series,What keeps me from growing. Lincoln, Nebraska: Good news Broadcasting Association.

Link, R. (2018, 07 30). 8 Health Benefits of Fasting, Backed by Science-

Healthline. Retrieved 03 03, 2021, from www.healthline.cvom: www.healthline.com/nutrition/fasting-benefits

Morris, P. R. (Director). (25/04/2012). Ten Deadly Sins [Motion Picture]. Online Publishing, Inc. (2010, 10 01). Power Bible CD. Bronson , Michigan, United States of America.

RR Micro Tech Solution. (2019, 04 02). Diseases dicttionary app. Chennai, Vellore, India.

Webster, N. (1828, 04 14). American Dictionary of the English Language. Retrieved 03 07, 2021, from webstersdictionary1828.com: webstersdictionary1828.com/

Wilson, D. (2016, 09 26). 10 Signs you love money. Retrieved 03 03, 2021, from www.crosswalk.com:

www.google.com/amp/s/www.crosswalk.com/family/finances/planning/10-signs-you-love-money.html%3famp=1